Chasm Of Death!

Lucy moaned and tried to struggle but Clint gripped her by her belt and shouted, "Hang on and don't move! Duke can't carry us both up this cliff fast enough to escape the Indians, and I can't let loose of you or you'll fall."

The lead warrior below fired an arrow that lanced meanly off the rock near their heads. Clint had to keep firing down at the warriors to keep them out of close arrow range.

At last the rim hove into sight, and Clint shouted, "We're going to make it! Don't give up, Lucy!"

"But look!"

Clint did look and what he saw made his blood run cold.

Also in THE GUNSMITH series

THE GUNSMITH

111

GRAND CANYON GOLD

JOVE BOOKS, NEW YORK

GRAND CANYON GOLD

A Jove Book/published by arrangement with
the author

PRINTING HISTORY
Jove edition/March 1991

ISBN: 0-515-10528-7

Jove Books are published by The Berkley Publishing Group,
200 Madison Avenue, New York, New York 10016.
The name "JOVE" and the "J" logo
are trademarks belonging to Jove Publications, Inc.

PRINTED IN THE UNITED STATES OF AMERICA

10 9 8 7 6 5 4 3 2 1

ONE

To Clint's way of thinking, Apache Junction had only one real attraction, and that was Miss Lucy Holland, owner of the Geronimo Saloon and Dancehall. Other than Miss Lucy, Apache Junction was just another Arizona boom town fed by gold, greed, and a few big cattle ranches. It was February, though, and the Arizona Territory was a good place to be wintering. To hell with places like Wyoming, Montana, and Colorado, where the temperatures froze a man's blood and the snows were deep.

Yes sir, Apache Junction suited Clint just fine. He'd opened a popular gunsmithing shop, which, while it would not make him rich, kept his hands occupied and brought in enough cash to pay for his hotel room, meals, and the board of Duke, his fine black gelding.

At five o'clock every afternoon, Clint would usher the last of his customers out the door, hang his CLOSED sign in the window, and then, washing his hands of gun oil, comb his hair and walk over to spend a few pleasant hours of conversation and cards at the Geronimo Saloon. About eight o'clock, he might talk Miss Lucy into joining him for dinner and a few drinks, and then he'd escort her back to her saloon and dancehall. If she was in the mood and

the crowd numbered more than twenty or thirty, Miss Lucy
would sing a few songs and dance on her stage, to the
delight of everyone. About midnight, Clint would wink
at Miss Lucy, and if she winked back, it meant that she
was interested in meeting him upstairs for a little pleasure.
And even if she didn't wink, Clint might just decide to
sweet-talk her into joining him for a moonlight stroll that
might well end up in his own hotel room.

Yes sir, Apache Junction was a good place to winter,
but the town itself wasn't much. In fact, to the Gunsmith's
way of thinking, Apache Junction was pretty raw. Most of
the three thousand or so inhabitants were miners, rough
sonsabitches who'd rather fight, drink, and fornicate than
anything else. They were the kind of men who'd work all
day long in some dark tunnel, risking their lives grubbing
for gold and silver, then take their daily three dollars in
hard-won wages and spend it all on whiskey, cards, and
wild women. Not that Clint disapproved, because his phi-
losophy was that it took all kinds of men to make the world
go around—even miners, who were not his favorite kind
of people.

"Say Clint," one of his customers said, "where in the
world did you get this beauty!"

Clint had been working on the firing pin of an old single-
shot Remington that had long since seen its prime. He
turned around to see a couple of cowboys hanging over
his glass display case. The Gunsmith did not have to look
at what had gotten the men so excited. It was, he knew,
a pair of pearl-handled Colt .45 Peacemakers that he'd
special-ordered from their manufacturer back in Hartford,
Connecticut.

"Pretty nice, aren't they," Clint said, for he understood
how men could admire that quality of firearms.

"Mind if we touch 'em?" one of the cowboys asked.

Clint could have refused the request, but the two young cowboys, neither of whom would probably ever be able to afford such a fancy pair of pistols, looked so longingly at the weapons that Clint simply did not have the heart.

Taking the pistols out of the case and removing them from their red-felt lined box, he handed each of the cowboys one of the weapons. "Just keep your hands off the bluing," he warned, "but you're sure welcome to feel the balance."

The cowboys held the guns almost lovingly. They brushed their work-roughed fingertips back and forth against the pearl handles.

"Prettiest things I ever held, except for the bare bottom of a young woman up in Prescott," one of the cowboys said.

"Whiter than a whore's tits, too," the other one said, swallowing noisily. "Mind if I cock it?"

"Go ahead." Clint said. "Just don't drop the hammer."

"Sure enough," the cowboy promised.

Clint stepped back and watched the young men. He enjoyed watching people enjoy themselves, whether they were lost in admiration of a woman, a horse, a gun, or a good saddle.

"You ought to keep them for yourself," one of the cowboys said, "you being a famous gunfighter and all. Yes sir, you just ought to keep and wear them."

"Not me," Clint said.

"Well, why not?"

Clint shrugged. "Oh, they're a little too fancy to my way of thinking. You'd expect a man like Wild Bill Hickok or Buffalo Bill Cody to come waltzing into a saloon wearing that kind of fancy get-up."

Clint patted his own worn but very well-used and cared-for sidearm. "I think of a gun as being a tool rather than an ornament. And a good tool—well, it's usually pretty plain."

The two cowboys stared at the gun on Clint's narrow hip. One of them blurted, "You ought to have at least kept some notches on the handle for all the men you've gunned down."

"Naw!" the other snorted. "Why, the Gunsmith has gunned down so many men that he'd have to whittle his gunbutt down to a nubbin' if he did that. Why, it'd look like a damn beaver had a meal of it!"

The two cowboys laughed at their little joke as they tested the balance of the pearl-handled Colts. "How much does a set of pistols like this run a man?" one of the cowboys finally asked.

Clint took the pistols and replaced them in their felt-lined case. "These are special commemorative pistols," he explained. "Colt only made a thousand of them. They'll cost $250.00—each."

"Whoo-wee!" one cowboy exclaimed. "Five hundred dollars! Why, that's a year's wages!"

"*Top* wages," his friend said.

Clint nodded and replaced the guns in his case. "They are fancy," he said, "and as fine a pair as I've ever seen. But the thing of it is, a pistol, no matter how fancy, is only as good as the man using it."

Clint shut the glass case and relocked it. "Now, you take those two old hawglegs you boys are wearing: They'll kill a man or a rattlesnake just as fast and as dead as those pearl-handled pistols. And a fancy gun, no matter how well balanced and made, won't make you shoot any straighter."

"That's true enough," one of the young cowboys admitted. "But I sure would like to have that set. Why, I can just see myself now, a-struttin' into the Geronimo Saloon or some whorehouse, and then watchin' the girls stare at me. They'd sure as hell know I was important with a set of guns like that!"

"They sure would," the other young cowboy said.

Clint frowned. "A set of guns like that is just for show," he explained. "No respectable gunfighter would take a man seriously who wore two such fancy weapons. And as for parading around in the saloons, you could just bet your bottom dollar that someone drunk and mean would take notice and start heckling you. He'd either want to see the guns, or maybe get you into a poker game and win them from you. And he might even challenge you to prove how fast you could use them."

Clint shook his head at the suddenly very somber pair. "I'll tell you this, my young friends: Those kinds of guns are all for show. You sure as hell would be asking for trouble if you wore them into a saloon."

"Guess you're right about that, Clint."

"I know I am," the Gunsmith said, seeing the large, heavyset outline of Mayor Wallace Boggs fill his open doorway.

Mayor Boggs was a big, slope-shouldered braggart in his early thirties. He liked to dress like a banker, with a black suit, hat, polished boots, starched white shirt, and black tie. Boggs wore the largest gold watch and chain Clint had ever seen. It was so large that the joke around Apache Junction was that you could snap the watch open and eat dinner on the inside of the cover.

"Howdy, boys," the mayor said, dismissing the cowboys with a glance and turning his full attention on the gun case. "Clint, I see you finally got those guns for me. It's about time. I don't know as what I'd order them locally again, seeing as how it took you over a month to receive the order."

"I told you it would be slow," Clint said, trying to keep from bristling at this overbearing lout. "And if I hadn't personally ordered them, you might not even have been able to receive this pair."

"Hell, don't give me that line of bullshit," the mayor snapped. "Get 'em out of the case for me."

Clint did as he was told because the mayor still hadn't completely paid for the guns. There was a twenty-five-dollar Wells Fargo special freight and service charge that had not been paid.

Clint removed the weapons from the case and put them down on the counter. Mayor Boggs snapped them up with a grin. He twisted and held the guns up to the window and turned them slowly in the sunlight.

"Damn they're pretty!" he said with a shake of his head. "Finest pair of matched pistols I've ever seen outside of a museum."

"They're special, all right," Clint said in agreement, as he thought about what a waste they were on this big, blustering politician.

"What about holsters?"

"I told you that Peter Raymond, the saddlemaker, would make you a fine pair," Clint reminded the mayor. "Did you ask him?"

"Naw," Boggs snapped. "I don't much care for Raymond. He's a prickly bastard. Always trying to tell people what they need instead of asking what they need. I never have liked that crotchety old man."

Clint glanced at the two young cowboys and he could read his own feelings reflected in their expressions. The pair knew saddles and leatherwork and that Raymond was the finest man with leather they'd ever seen and that his saddles had always commanded a premium in Arizona and would continue to do so for a hundred years after his death.

"Maybe you should ask old man Raymond to make me a set of holsters and a cartridge belt," the mayor snapped. "I don't see why you didn't do that. I'd give you an extra five dollars."

"He'd need to measure your waist and the length of your leg," Clint said, as the two cowboys departed with a scowl on their faces, which was just typical of the kind of reaction that Wallace Boggs generally created.

"Aw, to hell with that!" Boggs snapped. "Give me a tape measure and I'll give you the figures you need. Then you take them over to old man Raymond and have him make me a set of fancy matched holsters."

Clint shook his head. "No sir," he said. "I think I'll just pass up that easy money. If you want holsters, then you go over to Mr. Raymond and ask for them yourself."

The mayor's jaw dropped. "Are you refusing to help me? After the kind of commission you're probably getting on this deal from the Colt factory!"

"I'm taking a small commission," Clint said in a brittle voice. "No more and no less than I ordinarily get. And besides that, you owe me a twenty-five-dollar handling charge that I had to pay Wells Fargo because you were out of town on business."

"Twenty-five dollars!" the mayor cried. "Why, that's robbery! I won't pay it!"

Clint's hands flashed out, and he yanked the guns from Boggs's hands. "You'll pay me, all right, or I'll keep these."

Boggs was not one accustomed to being denied. "Clint Adams, you give me back those guns I paid for, or you'll be biting off more grief than you can imagine! This is *my* town, and I can get you run out of it!"

It was all Clint could do to whisper "On what charge?"

"Cheating your customers."

"I'm not cheating anyone!" Clint turned and went to a shoebox in which he kept his money, receipts, and records. The Wells Fargo receipt was right on the top of the stack.

"Here!" he said, slamming it down on the counter. "The receipt that proves I paid for the shipping and handling charges on those expensive pistols out of my own pocket. Now pay up, Boggs, or get the hell out of my shop!"

"Five hundred dollars was enough. Take your damn Wells Fargo money out of your commission!" the mayor shouted, slamming his fist down on the glass case so hard it was a wonder that it did not shatter.

Clint reached across the counter and grabbed Boggs by the shirtfront with his left hand and used his right to slap the man across the side of his jaw.

Boggs roared in anger and grabbed Clint's arm. The mayor stood well over six feet and weighed considerably in excess of two hundred pounds, so the next thing Clint knew, he was being jerked into his glass case.

"No!" Clint shouted, as the case toppled over and glass shattered across the floor. He and Boggs went reeling out the front door, across the boardwalk and into the street.

Clint shook the man's grip off, ducked a powerful right hand, and buried his left into the mayor's soft gut. The big man woofed like a sick dog and his face turned the color of a fish's belly. Boggs grabbed his aching stomach, and Clint brought his right fist up from his boottops. It exploded against the mayor's square jaw, and the man was knocked skidding across the dirt.

"Dammit, pay me!" Clint shouted, as people began pouring out into the street to watch.

Boggs shook his head. His lip was bleeding, and he staggered to his feet as Clint waded in on him. Boggs threw a few feeble punches, but Clint's blows had taken the heart out of the mayor. Clint hit the man twice more and he went down again. Before Boggs could shake off his haze, Clint reached inside the mayor's coat and removed his wallet. He counted out fifteen dollars and threw the wallet in the man's bloodied face.

"There, Mr. Mayor," he growled. "*Now* you only owe me ten dollars."

"I'll have you arrested and thrown in jail!" Boggs choked. "I'll have you sent to prison!"

Clint had started to turn away, but now he stopped, pivoted about, and studied the big man in his fancy clothes. "You try and imprison me and that'll be the worst mistake you've ever made."

Clint turned and headed back to his shop. Hell, he thought, the fifteen dollars he'd just extracted from Boggs wouldn't even replace his broken glass display case.

"I should have ground his damn out-sized watch under my bootheel in repayment," the Gunsmith growled.

TWO

"Here," Lucy Holland said, taking the broom from Clint's bruised hand, "you aren't worth a damn at sweeping up messes."

Clint nodded. His knuckles were bloodied and he was still madder than a teased snake because he was out a very expensive glass case. "I've always been a whole lot better at making messes than cleaning them up."

Lucy found a dustpan and gave it to Clint as she swept the glass into a single neat pile. She was a beautiful woman in her early thirties, with strawberry-blond hair, green eyes, and a pair of full lips and breasts.

"Don't just stand there staring at me," Lucy said. "Use the dustpan to help."

"Yeah," Clint said, kneeling down and using the dustpan, while Lucy swept the glass up so he could dump it into a trashcan. "You sure have pretty ankles."

She giggled like a schoolgirl. "You ought to know."

"Oh," he said, scooping up the last of the debris, "I do know. And I also know that what's upstairs from those shapely ankles is pretty nice."

"Just 'pretty nice'?" she asked, eyebrows arching in a question. He emptied his dustpan of glass and dropped it to the floor. The door to his gunsmithing shop was closed but it wasn't shuttered, so Clint had to be a little discreet. He maneuvered Lucy around so that he could slip his bruised left hand around her small waist and rub his right hand over the mound of her full breasts.

"It's *all* nice," he said, looking right into her eyes and hearing her sigh with pleasure, but then she pulled away.

"Stop it!" she said, straightening her blouse. "The whole damn town is probably watching."

It was dark outside and Clint could not be sure exactly how many people might actually be watching, so he stepped back. "What about us getting together a little later tonight?"

"I don't know," she said coyly. "You've already had quite a bit of excitement for one day."

"I think my heart could stand the strain of a little more."

"We'll see," Lucy told him, reaching behind her to open the door. "But I've got a saloon to run. It's Friday night."

Clint frowned. Lucy enjoyed his loving as much as any woman ever had, but she was all business when it came to making money. Clint had never seen a more ambitious lady. It was said that Miss Lucy Holland was the second-richest person in Apache Junction, right behind the mayor.

"What about dinner together in an hour or so?" he asked.

"I can't," she said. "Too much business tonight. You know as well as I do that it's payday on the ranches and most of the mines. I've got to go on stage and keep them in my establishment, or they'll go down the street to see other women."

"They won't see any half as pretty as you, though," Clint said.

She kissed him quickly. "You are a flatterer and a gentleman, Clint Adams. And if you were just a little richer, I'd marry you."

He laughed, because this was a joke between them. "I'm not rich at all. Besides, I hear that you're rich enough for the both of us."

Lucy reached back behind her and opened the door. "No one is ever rich enough," she said. "All I'm waiting for now is for my father to strike it rich somewhere out in the desert. I guess then I'll feel that I can take life easy."

"He's chasing dreams, Lucy. Every prospector I ever heard of spent his whole life chasing dreams. I like your father, but he's never going to strike it rich twice in a lifetime."

Lucy's pretty smile slipped. Her father, old Albert Holland, had struck a glory hole about seven years earlier. With a small fortune burning a hole in his pocket, he'd promptly bought the Geronimo Saloon. Two months later he'd gotten icy feet again, given the saloon to Lucy, and raced off with several of his old friends to San Francisco's wild Barbary Coast to squander the last of his money. Now he was broke, in debt to half the store owners in Apache Junction, but happy again, chasing his dreams of a second big strike somewhere out in the vast reaches of Arizona.

"My father *will* make another strike," Lucy announced. "And it will be bigger than the first one."

Clint smiled tolerantly. "As long as he's happy, what does it matter?"

"I guess you're right," Lucy said. "It doesn't matter. I've already salted enough money away to take care of him. He's too proud to come to me and ask for money, even though he gave me the Geronimo. He'd much rather borrow a grubstake from everyone in town. That way he sort of feels like everyone believes in him."

"So what," Clint asked, "are you going to do if he really

does strike it rich again and tries to pay off all of his new debts?"

"I don't know," Lucy admitted, "but I can worry about that when it happens."

She reached up and touched his cheek. "I'm glad you whipped Wally Boggs. Real glad, because he's been insufferable for too long. He's got a thing for me, you know."

"Everyone in Apache Junction has a 'thing for you,' " Clint said. "But I didn't know the mayor was high on that list."

"Well, he is," she said. "Once he actually tried to slip his hand into my blouse."

"Can you blame him?" Clint asked, reaching himself but getting his hand slapped as Lucy stepped outside.

"When I slapped his face, he told me he loved me."

Clint stopped grinning. "What a fool! Though I can understand his problem."

"No you can't," Lucy said. "You're a drifter. You may *tell* women you love them, but that smile and those eyes tell me that all you want to do is mount them."

"My, my," Clint said, "you certainly have me pegged right."

"You bet I do," Lucy said with a laugh. "The only trouble is, you're the best man I ever had make love to me."

"And that's a problem?"

"It is if you're worried about getting your heart broken."

Lucy blew him a kiss. "I'll see you later."

"Sure," Clint said as she walked away, hips swinging and the eyes of cowboys and miners alike popping with desire.

That evening, Clint went to the Geronimo just like always, and he was a celebrity. Every person he saw congratulated him on the sound whipping he'd given the mayor.

"That overstuffed sonofabitch has been parading around here too damn long," a miner groused, and his opinion was roundly seconded.

Clint glanced toward the stage, knowing that Miss Lucy would soon come out and do her usual song and dance. "Well," he said, "if everyone feels that way about Mayor Boggs, how come he got elected?"

"Damned if we can figure that out!" a bushy-faced miner stormed.

"Why, I can tell you," another man said. "It's because he bought the damn votes! Don't you boys remember that he was runnin' against old Abe Wheeler and buying everyone who voted for him free whiskey?"

The men grunted, and Clint could tell that they were a little too ashamed to admit that they had sold their votes.

"Well," a cowboy grunted as he tossed down a shot of rye, "I sure ain't going to vote for the bastard again—even if he promises me a whole damn bottle!"

"The hell you won't," another man snickered. "You'd sell your mother out for a whole bottle."

The cowboy, a tall man in his late twenties, tried to take a swing at his detractor, but he was restrained and his attention diverted when the crowd suddenly burst into catcalls and applause.

"Good evening, gentlemen!" Miss Lucy said, climbing up on the stage as her piano player began to finger the keys.

"Good evening, Miss Lucy!" the crowd roared in greeting, most of the men lifting their glasses in a toast.

"What would you like to hear tonight?" Lucy called down to the crowd of eager faces.

" 'Arizona Ladies'!" a huge miner shouted, and his vote

was seconded by many in the crowd, because it was one of the songs that Miss Lucy did best.

"All right," she said, smiling and bowing low enough so that the all-male audience could see all the way down to her navel. And there was so much to see that they burst out into cheers and whoops of appreciation.

Miss Lucy batted her long eyelashes at the crowd, signaled her piano player to strike up the song, and then began to tap her foot to the music.

Arizona women like tall handsome men with class,
    men with fists of steel and big balls of brass. . . .

The crowd hollered and stomped their feet in a frenzy of appreciation as Miss Lucy launched into the second stanza of her ribald ballad. Clint had a big grin on his face until a hand tapped him on the shoulder.

"Clint Adams?"

Clint turned to see Ulysses Timberman, the United States marshal, staring him in the face. Ulysses wore a black patch over his left eye and his left ear was missing, shot off in the same shotgun blast that had robbed him of half his vision. The man was of average size, but he somehow seemed very large. He was dirty, grim-faced, and feared as a lawman who would rather shoot a man than mess around with hauling him to jail.

"What do you want?" Clint said, forgetting about Lucy and tensing. Clint had never had a run-in with Marshal Timberman, but he'd always figured that, if he did, one of them would wind up dead. Timberman was just that kind of a man. He would not back down, no matter who he came up against.

"I got a warrant for your arrest."

"Arrest?" Clint scowled. "What are you talking about?"

"Why don't you come outside and I'll explain it to you?"

Clint nodded. "You first, Marshal."

Timberman didn't like going out first, but with the crowd and all, he decided that he could break a personal rule and turn his back on Clint.

As Clint followed the marshal toward the door, he tried to imagine what kind of a charge could have been leveled against him. The only thing he could come up with was that it had something to do with that fight he'd had with Mayor Boggs. Timberman pushed outside, and that's when Clint saw Boggs standing in wait, with a six-gun clenched in his fist.

"Oh no you don't," Clint said, stopping in his tracks and letting the batwing doors swing shut.

Timberman was back inside in less than five seconds. "What the hell is the matter with you!"

"I see a welcoming committee waiting outside, and I don't think that I'm going to walk through those doors unless you disarm our mayor."

Timberman's face flushed with anger. "I let you walk out without being handcuffed, Adams. But I won't stand for your resisting arrest."

"And I won't be gunned down by Wallace Boggs while you stand aside!"

Timberman's eyes sparked danger. His hand slipped down toward the butt of his gun.

"Marshal," Clint said, "I know you're a brave man, but I thought you were also a little smarter than to allow yourself to be forced into a gunfight. I didn't do anything to Boggs except demand and then take the payment that was owed to me. I still came out of the deal losing money, considering he smashed the hell out of my display case."

"You assaulted the mayor in public and you took his money by force," Timberman said stubbornly. "The mayor chooses to file charges against you, and it is my duty to carry them out. So you are under arrest."

"I've got a receipt from Wells Fargo that proves I was owed twenty-five dollars!"

"And the mayor has a receipt that says he was owed one pair of fancy Colt Peacemakers!"

Clint ground his teeth with frustration. "And what about my display case! It'll cost me a hundred dollars to have it replaced."

"I don't know a thing about that."

Clint glanced past the marshal and saw that several men had joined Boggs out in the street. He could not see them clearly because their faces were in shadow, but something told him that if he surrendered, he would go to jail and never live to see a courtroom.

"Marshal," he said, as the room became quiet and Miss Lucy's song died on her lips, "Marshal, I've spent most of my adult life upholding the law in little frontier towns like Apache Junction, and I've sort of developed a sixth sense for how to stay alive. And right now, that sixth sense tells me *not* to hand over my gun."

Ulysses Timberman took a deep breath and his hand shadowed his gunbutt. "In that case, I'm going to have to kill you."

Clint cursed silently. The very last thing in the world he wanted to do was to kill a United States marshal. Timberman was a fool, but he was also the only law across several thousand square miles of Arizona. To kill him— even to avoid a wrongful arrest—would be a terrible mistake. He'd be a wanted man, with a bounty on his head.

"Marshal," Clint said, using his left hand to gesture toward the crowd, "you can ask almost anyone in this place, and they'll tell you that I only took the fifteen dollars that was owed to me. And as for the matched pair of Peacemakers, I'll give them to the mayor if he'll make some restitution for my display case."

"You'll hand over your gun right now or face the consequences," Timberman said, not backing down at all.

Dozens of men started to complain that Clint was getting a raw deal, but the Gunsmith barely heard them. This hard-headed, one-eyed marshal was going to push him over the edge and force him into drawing his gun.

"Clint, no!" Lucy shouted, wedging herself between him and the marshal. "Don't! He's not worth it!"

"The mayor and a few of his friends are waiting outside," Clint said. "I just don't think I'll live to reach the jail. Do you, Marshal?"

Timberman flushed. "I make no promises."

"That's what I thought."

"Listen," Lucy pleaded, "we'll make the promises, won't we, boys? You can all see the way this game is rigged. Will you help me get Clint safely to jail and then see that he's not murdered while he awaits trial?"

The crowd shouted in agreement, but Clint was still not convinced. "This is dead wrong," he said stubbornly. "And besides, you can't watch over me night and day. They'll take my gun and I'll be at their mercy."

Lucy thought about that for a moment, then said, "Marshal, how about if I get arrested too?"

"What!"

"You heard me. I want to be arrested along with Clint."

Timberman was confused and upset. "Miss Holland, now you just get out of the way."

"No!" Lucy cried, and she reached back and swung her open fist to strike the marshal's cheek with a loud popping sound.

"Sonofabitch!" he shouted.

Lucy stepped back behind Clint for protection. "Am I under arrest for slapping a law officer?"

"You're damn right you are!"

"Good!" Lucy linked her arm through Clint's. "Then let's go to jail—and you'd better protect our lives, Marshal Timberman, or my customers will see that we get justice."

"Damn right we will!" a big miner shouted.

Timberman surveyed the crowd, and to Clint, the man looked suddenly very worried. Timberman was brave, but he was not a quick or a deep thinker, and Clint suspected that events had just totally gotten out of the marshal's hands.

"All right," Timberman said, turning and yelling out the door. "Major, you and those men just get the hell off the street. I'm bringing Clint Adams and Miss Lucy Holland out, and they're going to jail."

"Miss Lucy!" Boggs shouted. "What the hell are you arresting *her* for!"

"For assaulting a law officer. Now Boggs, you do as I say, or I'll arrest you too!"

The mayor cursed, but they all saw him and his friends walk up the street until they disappeared from view.

"Clint, hand over your six-gun and let's go." Timberman snarled.

Clint reluctantly gave the marshal his gun. "I think we're making a big mistake," he said to Lucy.

"Not as big a mistake as you'd have made if you'd killed this fool."

"I guess you're right about that," Clint said, as he allowed the marshal to take his arm and escort him out of the Geronimo.

With half the adult male population in attendance, Clint

and Lucy were marched down the street into the sheriff's office, then put into a cell. Apache Junction had hired a succession of sheriffs, but they'd either been run off or planted in the cemetery, until no one would take their places. That's why the only law in town was that administered by Ulysses Timberman.

"When is the judge coming through town next to hold court?" Clint asked, as the jail door was slammed shut behind him and Lucy.

"Monday."

Clint nodded. Well, at least they would not have to wait too long to explain things to the judge and then be released.

Lucy was staring at the single hard wooden bench. "Where's the bed?"

"Ain't no bed," Timberman grunted, with a thin smile of triumph. "Prisoners sleep on the floor."

"The hell you say!" Clint raged. "Miss Lucy isn't sleeping on a hard rock floor."

"She can sleep on her feet, on the bench, or on you," Timberman growled, "but she asked to be arrested, and damned if she isn't going to face the consequences."

"Well, can you at least bring us some blankets?" Clint raged. "And how about some water and a couple of pillows?"

Timberman walked over to his own cot. "Sorry," he said in a mocking voice, "but I just plain don't have the money to provide prisoners with all the niceties of life. Real pity, ain't it?"

"You miserable bastard!" Clint said, outraged that a woman like Lucy should have to suffer hardships. "I should have gunned you down in the Geronimo like you deserve."

The mockery went out of Timberman's expression. "You could have tried," he said, "but I'm pretty fast with a gun myself. And I've killed men with reputations like yours. Most often I find that they've lost their nerve after they retire from the business of killing. I suspect that you're no different."

Clint's expression was murderous. "Some day, Marshal, I'll make sure you have another chance to test that theory."

"We'll see about that," Timberman said, stretching out on his cot and closing his one eye. "We'll just see."

THREE

Marshal Timberman had slept no more than fifteen minutes when the front door of his office burst open and a dozen rough, drunken miners and cowboys overwhelmed him.

To his credit, Timberman put up a spirited fight, but sheer numbers overwhelmed and disarmed him. The keys to the jail cell were found hanging on a peg, and while Clint and Lucy watched, the citizens of Apache Junction opened the cell and raised their bottles in a rousing cheer.

"To justice!" a burly miner shouted.

"To justice!" the crowd roared, as the men rushed inside to pull the startled prisoners out.

Ulysses Timberman was being held down by a pile of drunken men. Thrashing and cursing, he yelled, "I'll arrest the whole damn lot of you!"

A miner looked over at Clint. "What shall we do with him?"

Clint considered the question. He was afraid that if he let Timberman free, the man would be so angry he'd get a gun and start blazing away, maybe killing innocent people.

"Put him in the cell," Clint said. "Sleeping without blankets will cool him off in a hell of a big hurry."

Lucy nodded with satisfaction. "We'll just leave him there until Judge Stallings arrives, and he can figure out what to do with him."

Clint figured that was a damn good idea. Timberman would have three cold days in the spartan cell to reflect upon the error of his ways. By the time Monday rolled around, the lawman might be a little more reasonable and easier to deal with.

It took four strong men to drag a kicking and hollering Timberman into the jail cell and then get the door closed behind him. He was like a caged cougar, hissing and screeching curses. He spit, cursed, and kicked at the bars and the men with such demented ferocity that he sobered the crowd.

"That sumbitch is crazy," a miner said to no one in particular. "He's the one that should be imprisoned before he kills someone."

"You got that right," Clint said, taking Lucy's arm and escorting her outside.

"Drinks are on the house at my place!" Lucy shouted at the top of her voice.

The crowd cheered and surged back down the street toward the Geronimo Saloon and Dancehall.

"It's been quite a night, hasn't it?" Clint said to Lucy.

"It's been one hell of a night," she replied. "I'm just a little worried about Ulysses Timberman. I'm afraid that this will humiliate him so badly that he'll come gunning for you the moment he gets out of jail."

"If he does," Clint said philosophically, "then I'll have no choice but to try and stop him permanently."

"But that will make you a wanted man," Lucy said with a sad shake of her head, "so that even if you won, you'd still lose."

"What do you know about this Judge Stallings? Is he fair or is he also reaching into the mayor's pockets whenever he dispenses the law?"

"He's a good man," Lucy said. "He used to be a prospector before he went back east to study the law. He's jailed my father many times for drunken and disorderly conduct, but he's always posted his bail and then grubstaked him. Judge Stallings will see that things are done according to the law."

Clint was relieved. "In that case, maybe we can make a good case for having Timberman stripped of his marshal's badge. It's clear that the man is unstable and on Mayor Boggs's payroll."

"I know that," Lucy said, "and so do you, but we don't have any evidence to support our accusation."

"Yeah," Clint reluctantly admitted, "I'm afraid you're right about that. But between now and the time that the judge arrives, maybe I can dig up some evidence against the marshal."

"How?"

"I don't know," Clint said, "but someone like Timberman will have made a lot of enemies, and they'll be more than happy to help convince a judge that Timberman ought to be stripped of his badge and thrown in jail for a long, long time."

Lucy nodded and squeezed the Gunsmith's arm tightly. "The boys are expecting a few songs," she said, "but after I'm finished, why don't you meet me upstairs in my room for a little champagne and loving?"

"Nothing I'd rather do," Clint said happily. "This night started off all wrong, but I think it's going to work out just fine."

"Better than 'fine,' " Lucy said, as the miners began to cheer and stomp their feet.

Clint eased forward to the bar and ordered a whiskey, then hooked his bootheels over the brass rail and leaned back to watch Miss Lucy sing and dance a little. Whirling and belting out another ribald tale, she had the crowd cheering and laughing, hollering and applauding.

Lucy gave them five songs, and every one of them was better than the last. She had four bartenders trying to keep up with pouring free drinks during her performance, and when it was over, the crowd would drink the Geronimo Saloon empty before they staggered out at dawn.

Clint slipped away and headed for the back room where Lucy lived. He ducked into the room and barely had time to remove his hat before Lucy came rushing inside, with a wave of thunderous applause following her down the hallway.

"Lock the door," Lucy said, raising a bottle of champagne. "Tonight we're going to celebrate."

"What's the occasion?"

"Do we really need one?"

Clint locked the door and turned back to see the woman coming into his arms. "I don't think we do," he said as his lips crushed hers.

Lucy was hot from her dancing and singing, and when they broke their embrace, Clint opened the champagne and poured into the crystal glasses she extended.

"To love and money," Lucy said, raising her glass.

"To lovin' and livin'," Clint added.

Clint set his glass down and reached for Lucy, who melted into his arms. A moment later, they were fumbling at each other's snaps, buckles, and buttons as they hurriedly stripped out of their clothing, yanked the bedspread and blankets aside, then jumped into Lucy's large, soft bed.

Clint buried his face between Lucy's generous breasts,

and when she moaned with pleasure and began to stroke his buttocks, he raised his head and used his tongue on her nipples until they were as firm and upstanding as gumdrops.

"Oh, yes," she breathed, her fingers slipping between their bodies to caress Clint's throbbing manhood.

Clint pushed Lucy's shapely legs wide apart and let her guide his big rod to her moist honeypot. Lucy rubbed his manhood up and down between her legs until she was squirming with pleasure and Clint was unable to keep his hips from moving.

"Come on," she whispered, guiding him into her wetness, "do it to me!"

Clint was only too happy to oblige. He had had more than his share of beautiful and passionate women, but none had ever fired his passion the way that Lucy could. She was like a cat, long and slick and purring, and his manhood began to thrust in and out of her hard body. Then the kitten turned into a tiger.

"Harder!" she cried, her heels working up and down on the sheets, her fingernails raking his back with a terrible, driving urgency.

Clint's body moved over her with an expertise born of great experience. Soon Lucy's hips were thrusting powerfully at him, and her head was rolling back and forth with passion.

"Oh yes!" she cried, straining to bring them both to a climax. "Don't stop! Don't even slow down!"

Clint could not have stopped if he tried. He was also out of control, and when he began to jerk and fill Lucy with his seed, she locked her legs around behind his back and lost herself in her own release, bucking and humping like a wild young filly.

For a long time they lay locked together, the woman's

legs tight around Clint's lower back, her hips pulsating strongly, milking Clint dry.

"That was wonderful," she sighed at last, her legs dropping back to the bed, her face covered with a sheen of perspiration.

"You're the best I ever had," he told her. "You were made to satisfy a man, completely."

"Do you really mean it?" Lucy studied his face in the lamplight.

"I mean it," Clint said.

Lucy giggled like a schoolgirl and ran her fingers through his hair. "Don't you think that we'd make a wonderful pair?"

"Sure," he said. "We are great together."

"Not just like this," she said, "but you know . . . permanent."

Clint rolled off the woman. He sat up and reached for the champagne bottle and glasses. "You're not going to talk about marriage again, are you? Cause you've already told me that I'm not rich enough to marry."

"I was only kidding," she said, taking a glass and studying him thoughtfully. "Besides, in a few more years, I'll be rich enough to carry the both of us the rest of our days. I could sell the Geronimo, and we could go to California and retire."

"Now, why would we want to do a thing like that?"

"I thought you didn't like Apache Junction."

"It's fine," Clint said, then added, "for wintering."

"Well, that's what I mean. We could go to California, where the winters are also mild. We could buy a cottage near the coast and walk the beaches. You ever walk hand in hand with a beautiful woman along a sandy beach, Clint?"

"No, but I've walked with you across the desert at sundown, when the clouds were firing the sky and the air was soft and warm. I don't see how walking could get much more pleasant than that."

She hugged him. "Well, it's nice of you to say, but I'd like to walk the beach and hunt for shells. You know, I've never seen the ocean. Never."

"It's big," he said.

She studied his ruggedly handsome face, using her fingertip to trace the faint scar across his left cheek that served only to give his face more character. "I think we should get married and walk the beach some day."

Clint tossed down his champagne. "I think we should drink the rest of this champagne and make love again."

"So soon?"

Clint stroked her full breasts and then licked one nipple, making it wet with the taste of champagne. The nipple hardened almost instantly. "I can see that you're ready and willing."

"With you," Lucy said, stroking his thigh, "I'm *always* ready and willing."

Clint set his glass down and rolled her back into bed. There were going to be some problems to face in the morning with Timberman and the mayor, but to hell with it. Tonight, he was going to grab, root, and growl!

FOUR

The next morning Clint went to his gunsmith shop, fully expecting trouble from Mayor Boggs, but the big man did not show his face. Clint moseyed over to the sheriff's office to find Marshal Timberman ranting and raving about how he was going to kill the Gunsmith. After just a few minutes of listening to that kind of talk, Clint took his leave and went back to work.

About noon, one of the mayor's hirelings dropped by the gunsmith shop with ten dollars and a demand for the matched Peacemakers.

"Take the money back and tell Boggs he has to come pay me himself. I want a receipt for those pistols, and he's the only one that I'll have sign it."

The hireling stomped off, and several hours later, Boggs himself arrived, but he was not alone.

"You've bought yourself a one-way ticket to prison," the mayor snarled. "When the judge arrives, I'll see that he issues an arrest warrant, and if Timberman wants to deputize me and some of my men, then we'll agree. Either way, you're past history here in Apache Junction."

"Just sign for the receipt of the guns and pay me for the display case."

"What!"

"Be a hundred and ten dollars altogether," Clint said. "Cash."

Boggs blanched, looking as if he'd swallowed a big chicken bone, but in the end, he paid the bill and took the matched Colts. "I think I might use these for someone very special," he said.

Clint could not miss the man's true meaning. "If you think those fancy guns will make you man enough to brace me, you're an even bigger fool than I thought."

Boggs stomped out the door.

On Sunday, Clint and Lucy rented a horse and buggy and took a nice ride out into the country. It was interesting to look around, because you could see all the mines in operation. The damn things never shut down, and many of the miners who worked all week for the big mines would spend the day drinking and working their own pitiful claims.

One such man, old Zeke Matthews, hailed their buggy and motioned them to come over for a visit.

"Zeke one of your father's old friends?" Clint asked.

"He sure is," Lucy said as they drove closer.

Zeke was a tall, angular man in his midsixties. The lower half of his face was covered by a white beard, and because he was missing almost all of his teeth, his long hooked nose seemed to almost meet his prominent chin when he talked.

"Miss Lucy!" he cried, walking stiffly up to the buggy. "If you ain't a sight for these poor old eyes! Why I swear, you're prettier every time I see you!"

Lucy reached down and took the old miner's rough hand. She looked into Zeke's watery blue eyes. "How's the claim paying out these days?"

Zeke shook his head sorrowfully. "Miss Lucy, I'm afraid that lady luck is just passin' me by. I ain't gotten but a couple of bits worth of gold dust out of that danged old hole in the dirt."

Lucy had grown up hearing this sad refrain. She nodded sympathetically. "You look a little thin, Zeke. Aren't you eating enough to do the work?"

"Oh, sure I am!" the old man exclaimed, jumping back and shaking his head. "Why, I'm strong as a horse! Been eatin' just fine."

But even as he made that staunch declaration, Clint noticed how wobbly and weak he seemed.

"Well," Lucy said, "I am glad to hear that. But listen, I got a little extra money that I'd like to use to grubstake one of the best miners in Arizona. Of course, I'd hope that maybe you could try another hole, but . . . "

Zeke beamed. "Why, I just happen to have been thinkin' that maybe what I ought to do is try another claim! Course, it might not be any better'n this one, but . . . "

"Oh, I know there's never a guarantee," Lucy said quickly. "Don't forget, I'm a prospector's daughter. So I don't ever expect any return on a grubstake. But you never know. The very next claim you file might just turn up solid gold."

This was the kind of talk that a lifelong prospector like Zeke lived to hear. "Why, that's just true enough!" he shouted, the dullness of defeat washing away under the light of optimism.

The old man turned and used a bent forefinger to point toward a distant ridge of purple mountains. "You see those?"

"Why sure," Lucy said.

"Them's called the Juniper Mountains. I've been over them with your pa many a time. And though we never struck gold there, I got a strong feeling just lately that that's where a fortune lies."

"Really?"

"Yes, ma'am! The Junipers just has the look and the feel of gold! Now, all I'd need is a burro and some grub, maybe some new mining tools and a canteen that don't leak."

"For a half share, you've got all of that and whatever else you need," Lucy said with a soft smile.

The old man's eyes burned with joy and appreciation. "Why, you are an angel!" he cried. "I'll just drop this worthless old dig right this very moment and ride on back to Apache Junction in that buggy, if you don't mind."

"We'd be pleased to have your company, old-timer," Clint said. "And I'll even give you a hand loading up whatever you want to take back to town."

"That'd be real nice of you," Zeke said, hobbling off toward his camp.

When he was out of earshot, Clint said, "Are you sure that he's strong enough to go clear out there to the Junipers? He looks bone-tired and weak to me."

"Oh," Lucy said, "he's both of those things, but I'll have him put up for a couple of weeks in that hotel you're staying at. We'll fatten and rest him up, and he'll be good as new. I know these kind of men: Give them a grubstake and a little rest and they blossom like desert flowers after a spring rain."

Clint climbed down from the buggy, handing the reins to Lucy. "You are an angel of mercy," he said. "What you're doing for that old man is the same as giving him money."

"No," Lucy corrected, "if I tried to give him money, he'd refuse. But if I give him a grubstake and demand half interest, then I've given him hope and dignity."

"I see what you mean," Clint said as he went to help old Zeke gather up his few pitiful belongings to be loaded into the buggy and returned to Apache Junction.

Altogether, Clint didn't see five dollars worth of value in everything that the old prospector owned. It sure wasn't much to show for a lifetime of chasing golden dreams; but then Zeke was a man who'd spent his years exactly as he'd wanted, and that was worth plenty.

"Let's go," Lucy said, handing the reins to Clint as they turned the buggy around and headed back to town.

"Zeke," Clint said, glancing across the driver's seat, "there's a sandwich in that picnic basket that we didn't eat. It's yours if you're hungry."

The old prospector shook his head. "Naw, I ate not too long ago."

"Are you sure?" Lucy asked. "If you don't want it, we'll have to throw it out for the coyotes."

"Oh hell," Zeke said quickly, "if you're going to do that, I guess I could eat it."

Lucy got the sandwich out for the man and also a pitcher of beer. In less than a minute, both were inhaled by the famished prospector, though Lucy and Clint pretended not to notice.

Just outside of town, Lucy said, "Zeke, I haven't heard from Father in more than three months. Do you have any idea which direction he went off in this time?"

"Yep. He went northwest. He went to the Grand Canyon of the Colorado."

Both Lucy and Clint knew of it because Fort Yuma on the Colorado River had been a busy and important military post since the early 1850s. And several years before, Major John Powell had completed a daring exploration of the Colorado all the way from the Green River in Wyoming to the Virgin River in Nevada. Newspapers all over the United States had reprinted the account of his hair-raising navigation of the Grand Canyon.

"Now why would he go there?" Lucy asked.

Zeke didn't answer right away. He sucked on the dregs of his beer, squinted into the fading light of day, and then he wiped his nose on his ragged sleeve and said, "To find a lost Spanish fortune, I'd expect."

"A Spanish fortune?"

"That's right," Zeke said, his eyes distant and yearning. "I'm surprised he never said nothing to you, Miss Lucy. But then, he'd only just heard about it when I saw him heading out for that far country with old Shorty."

"Why didn't you go with them?" Clint asked out of curiosity.

"Well," Zeke said, "I was feelin' a little poorly when your father came through. Old Al, now he would have waited on me to get better, but I told him I had a claim of my own and was happy with the way the dirt looked. I was thinkin' that I'd strike it rich pretty quick. Course, I didn't."

Zeke's self-deprecating smile died and he added, "And then too, I heard bad stories of the Grand Canyon."

"What stories?" Lucy asked with alarm.

Zeke, realizing his mistake, tried to downplay his remark. "Aw, you know, just them same old stories. Most all they are, Miss Lucy, is superstitions anyhow. I don't hold them in much regard."

But Lucy was not to be put off, now that her fears were aroused. "Don't you dare hold back what you know! Now you tell me, Zeke! Tell me everything you heard about the Grand Canyon and that Spanish fortune."

Clint glanced sideways to see the old prospector squirming in his seat. He'd erred, and now there was no way out of the fix he'd gotten himself into except to tell everything. Lucy could be relentless, and the old prospector knew it.

"Well," Zeke said slowly, "the rumor is that the native

Indians that live in that great canyon are pretty mean. They sort of live down in there, and no one has ever civilized them or even been down to see them since some Spaniards descended into the canyon several hundred years ago in order to get water. I guess the Spaniards were all wiped out except for one who was spared, in order to teach the Indians how to use the muskets and weapons of the dead Spanish explorers."

Lucy glanced sideways at Clint. She looked very worried.

"Hear him out," Clint advised.

"Not much else to tell," the prospector said. "The Spaniards, according to popular legend, had a lot of gold with them when they went down into the Grand Canyon. The Indians took and hid the stuff in caves. No one has ever been able to find it, and those that have tried haven't come back."

"Oh, my God!" Lucy exclaimed. "Why would my father go into such a dangerous place?"

"He needs one more strike," Zeke explained. "Just one more, and he knows that he ain't got but a few more years than I do. So when he met a descendant of the Spaniard and the man was dying, your father helped save his life, and in return, the Indian agreed to help your father find the Spanish fortune."

"And he believed that story!"

"I believed it too," Zeke said quietly. "And like I said, if I hadn't been damn sick at the time and pretty sure that my own claim would pay off big, I'd have gone along with your father and old Shorty."

Lucy clenched her hands so tightly together that her knuckles were white. "Zeke, how far is it to the Grand Canyon?"

"Damned if I know. A couple hundred miles at least."

"Could you take me there?"

"What!"

"You heard me!"

Zeke swallowed noisily. "Miss Lucy," he began, "I don't know what happened to your father. Maybe nothing. But I do know that going off to that great canyon is not what he'd want me to help you do. It's hard, dangerous country out there."

Lucy nodded and stared at her clenched hands. "I'm sure that it's very hard country, Zeke. But I can't just remain in Apache Junction forever, waiting and wondering about my father. Maybe he needs my help!"

Clint shook his head. "Maybe he's already on the way back to us. Why don't you give him another week or two? If he isn't back by then . . . "

Clint didn't finish his sentence because he wasn't sure exactly what could be done. The Grand Canyon was said to be one of the world's greatest natural wonders. It was a deep, jagged gash in the earth that ran on for hundreds of miles, the result of the Colorado River cutting a pathway for thousands of years. The idea of even locating a single man in that vast earthen gutter was beyond comprehension.

"I don't know if I can wait," Lucy said.

"If you wait," Clint told her, "and he still hasn't come back in two weeks, then maybe Zeke will be strong enough to lead us to the Grand Canyon."

Lucy turned and gripped Clint's arm. "Then you'll come along too?"

"I couldn't live with myself if I let you go off without me," Clint heard himself say. "But I'm afraid our chances of finding your father and his friend would be very, very slim."

"Maybe not so slim," Zeke said.

Clint turned toward the man instantly. "What is that supposed to mean?"

"Just that Al drawed me a map and told me to come along if I changed my mind."

"He did!" Lucy almost bounced up and down on the seat. "And you still have it?"

Zeke's face fell with disappointment. "I'm afraid I lost it someplace."

"Oh no! Any chance we could go back to your claim and find it?"

"Nope. I already tried. Musta blew away in that dust storm we had a few weeks back. But I still sorta remember the map."

"If you had a piece of paper and a pencil, could you reproduce it?" Clint asked.

"You mean draw it again from memory?"

"Yes."

Zeke frowned mightily. "Well, sir. Maybe I could, but maybe I couldn't. My mind, she ain't as sharp as she was when I was your age."

"But you've got to at least try!" Lucy exclaimed. "My father's life may depend on it! Shorty's too!"

"I'll try, Miss Lucy. But I dunno. I'll just try."

Lucy squeezed the old prospector's arm. "You just think about it all the way back to Apache Junction. As soon as we get there and you've had a chance to eat a real meal and then rest up a little, I want you to sit down at the desk and try to draw that map of my father's from your memory."

"I'll do my best," Zeke said, without sounding very hopeful. "I remember that there was this river that fed into the canyon. Your pa, he mentioned it again and again."

Clint was not encouraged. "There must be hundreds of

rivers that feed into that mighty canyon."

"But this one," Zeke said, "was special. It was bright red, like blood, and it sliced through a pair of humped red mountains. And down near the river's shore, just before it reached the Colorado, there was an ancient Indian burial site. And Al said he saw something he'd never forget."

"What?" Lucy asked in a strained voice.

"A suit of Spanish armor girding the trunk of a juniper tree. He said the armor was beginning to split because the tree had grown so big. Said he'd never seen anything like that armor with a tree growing out its neck hole and branches out its arms."

The way Zeke described it made the hair stand up on the back of Clint's neck. "Well," he said finally, "that ought to be an easy landmark to spot."

Lucy nodded her head firmly, but her pretty face was very pale.

FIVE

On Monday, Judge Templeton J. Stallings arrived on the noon stage from Tucson. Clint and Lucy were there to meet him, but just as they started to come forward to introduce themselves, Mayor Boggs intruded.

"Well, Judge Stallings, good to see you, as always! How was your trip?"

The judge was a tall, spare man, with muttonchop whiskers, a high forehead, and piercing brown eyes. He was puffing on a briar pipe, and when he disembarked from the stage to be instantly confronted by the mayor, even Clint could tell that he was not pleased by the overexuberant greeting.

"The journey was, as always at this time of year, cold and unpleasant. I very much look forward to the day that I can retire in comfort. This circuit court business is not a bit to my liking."

Mayor Boggs's smile was frozen on his face. "Well, I can sure understand that. It's a hard country, filled with desperate and hard men. Allow me to take your valise and buy you a drink and lunch at the Elkhorn Club, sir."

Clint was not sure whether or not the judge would have accepted Boggs's offer, and before he had a chance to find out, Miss Lucy was pushing her way between the two men and grabbing the judge's hand.

"Judge, how good to see you again! The Elkhorn serves bad whiskey, so why don't you come over to my establishment and I'll pour you a round of the best in the house!"

The judge was a stern-faced man, but when he looked down into Lucy's pretty face, the corners of his thin lips actually curved into what Clint supposed was his best smile.

"Why Miss Holland, it is good to see you again! How is your father?"

"He's off chasing gold dust, as usual," Lucy said sweetly. "Won't you come along and I'll tell you all about him. But first, I want you to meet Mr. Clint Adams, a good friend of mine."

Boggs tried to interrupt, but the judge cut him off in midsentence. "Are you also known as the Gunsmith?"

"Yes," Clint said. "I've even opened a little gunsmithing business here for the winter."

"My, my!" Judge Stallings said. "I had supposed that you would be a much older man, given all the stories I've heard about your heralded law career."

"Dime novels," Clint said. "They do tend to exaggerate a bit, don't they?"

The judge smiled even wider. "That they do! And yes, it would be a pleasure to sit with you. I do, however, have to see what is on my docket in Apache Junction. Usually just a few simple cases of drunkenness and disorderly conduct."

Boggs was positively livid. "That's what I wanted to talk to you about over lunch, Judge! The Gunsmith was forcibly liberated from our jail by a drunken mob, and then poor Marshal Ulysses Timberman was thrown into his own cell!"

Judge Stallings cocked one of his caterpillar eyebrows and studied Clint. "Is this true, Mr. Adams? I find it almost inconceivable that a man of your reputation would allow such a thing to happen to a fellow law officer in need."

"I'm afraid Marshal Timberman was all fixed to set me up for an early grave," Clint explained.

"The hell he was!" Boggs roared. "You cheated and assaulted me, and the marshal was simply carrying out his orders!"

Stallings removed the briar pipe whose stem he was so adept at talking around, and he jabbed the stem at Boggs. "Mayor, a man in your public position ought to be familiar enough with the law and the rules of government to understand that a United States marshal like Ulysses Timberman does not take orders from anyone except the government, whose law it is he has sworn to uphold."

Boggs, caught off balance and publicly castigated, struggled to protest, but, under the judge's stern glare, he wilted.

"Well, sure," he said lamely, "I know that. But Adams broke the law, and I simply informed Timberman of the circumstances and he took it upon himself to make the arrest. And then the whole damn town got involved and justice was thwarted."

Boggs swallowed. "I'm confident that, when you hear the circumstances, you'll take strong and decisive measures to see that the Gunsmith is sent to prison."

Judge Stallings turned to Clint. "I am *not* going to hold court in the street," he announced. "So I want you to appear at the courthouse in two hours, prepared to explain to me what this is all about."

Boggs was astonished. "What about Marshal Timberman! He's locked in jail!"

The judge frowned. "I will speak to him right now.

Unfortunately, the marshal has a very bad temper, and I fear he might actually want to kill Mr. Adams before I can hear the circumstances behind this mess."

"He'll get a gun and come right after me the moment he is set free," Clint said. "I'll have to protect myself, Judge. Why don't we have the hearing at the sheriff's office, where the marshal can be kept safe behind bars? If it's your decision that I should be jailed instead of Ulysses Timberman, then I'll submit to the court."

"Judge," Boggs cried, "this isn't right! You can't hold court with a United States marshal locked in a cell!"

"I can hold court in a damn privy if I want to," the judge snapped. "Now, what the Gunsmith says makes sense. And seeing as how I know how Timberman thinks and acts, I figure that the Gunsmith is right. Justice can't be served if we have a damn shootout before I hear the facts of this confusing matter."

Lucy slipped her arm through that of the judge. "I think you're acting very wisely, Judge. As you always do. Now, can I buy you that special brand of whiskey you've been known to enjoy so much on your visits to Apache Junction?"

"Indeed you can, Miss Holland," the judge said, smacking his lips with anticipation as he and Lucy started for the Geronimo Saloon and Dancehall. "Indeed you can."

"Sonofabitch!" Boggs raged, yanking off a very expensive derby and slamming it to the ground, then kicking it high into the air.

Clint grinned wolfishly. "Sorry it didn't work out this time, Mayor. But you'll have your chance in two hours."

"The hell I will! By then Miss Holland will have that smitten old fool so twisted around her finger that he'll rule whichever way she wants."

"I guess in that case, you'll be out of luck," Clint said

with a straight face as he turned and went after Miss Lucy and the judge.

Two hours later they were gathered in the sheriff's office, and Marshal Timberman had to be ordered to keep his mouth shut or the hearing would be moved and he'd have no say whatsoever.

Miss Lucy stated the facts of the matter, and Clint gave his version. Mayor Boggs and the marshal, of course, had their own version; but, watching the judge, Clint didn't think the old man believed much of what they said.

"I rule that this matter has been settled and must remain settled," the judge said at last. "That means there is no money due to anyone and that you, Marshal—if you can keep a lid on that murderous temper of yours—will be released from that cell, but only on the condition that you drop your unwise intention to arrest the Gunsmith."

"But dammit, Judge, I can arrest anyone I damn well please!" Timberman stormed. "I've got the authority and the badge to do that!"

"No!" Stalling's eyes burned into the marshal's. "Private citizens cannot be arrested without due cause, and you had no cause to arrest Mr. Adams, except your desire to carry out the wishes of Mr. Boggs. The law simply does not work that way, Timberman. And if you don't understand that much, then I will see that your commission as a marshal is revoked."

Timberman blinked and paled a little. It seemed obvious to Clint that the threat of losing his authority was the only real thing that the marshal feared. The judge, knowing the man best, had also seen this and made the appropriate threat.

"This just ain't fair!" Timberman hissed, shaking with anger as the cell was unlocked.

Clint's hand moved toward his gun. If Timberman came at him again, he was going to pistol-whip the crazy fool and be done with him.

But Timberman did not charge Clint. Instead he stormed outside, with the mayor close on his heels.

"Thank you, Judge," Clint said.

"You're most welcome," Stallings said, "but I'm afraid that, knowing Ulysses Timberman, this is just the beginning of your troubles. He is a brave man and one that is relentless in the pursuit of criminals, but he is also out of control and ruthless. I think you might actually find it wise to leave Apache Junction."

"We are leaving," Lucy said. "We're going to find my father, if he doesn't show up very soon."

"Where is he now?"

"We think he and another prospector went to find a Spanish fortune in the Grand Canyon of the Colorado," Clint said.

"Really!" The judge was very interested in this piece of news. "I wonder if the fortune he seeks once belonged to Señor Garcia Lopez de Cardenas, who discovered that great canyon more than three hundred years ago."

"He did?" Clint asked.

"Why of course!" the judge exclaimed. "It is record-ed history that Señor Cardenas, under the great Spanish explorer Francisco Coronado, actually descended into the canyon, but he faced stiff opposition from the local Indians. I believe he needed water and left a company of soldiers to protect some of his supplies. Anyway, the soldiers were all annihilated by the Indians, and there were some who believed a fortune was lost. But of course, Cardenas was far too shrewd to admit this, because he and Coronado always planned to return and exact revenge on the Indians who had slaughtered their men."

"But they never did," Lucy said.

"That's correct," the judge said. "How did you know? Are you also a student of Southwestern history?"

"Not exactly," Lucy said, "but the story just fits that told my father, and it's the reason why he ventured so far into such dangerous territory."

"Your father is almost my age," the judge said, a hint of admiration but also of admonishment in his voice. "He should be sitting out in front of your saloon, enjoying the good weather and your fine whiskey."

"Oh, he does that when he's around," Lucy said, "but what he really loves is the hunt for gold. And the adventure."

The judge smiled. "Of course he does! Still, I'm greatly concerned that he bit off more than he can handle this time. That country surrounding the Grand Canyon is said to be wild and dangerous. And how would you ever find him?"

"We think that we have a map," Clint said, referring to Zeke and the map he'd drawn up in his room, with the red river and red hills. "We think we can find the place where Al Holland would have gone."

"Needle in a haystack," the judge said as they entered the saloon.

Clint had to agree. He sure hoped that Lucy's old prospecting father showed up in the next week or two. The Grand Canyon and all that wild country was sure as hell no place to go for a winter's vacation.

SIX

Al Holland was a very tall and a very thin old man. He was also extremely tired and worried as he and his prospecting partner, Shorty Mike, lay gasping on the snow-crusted southern rim of the Grand Canyon. In their bloodied hands they clenched battered Winchester rifles, and in their pockets rested six pieces of Spanish gold. But the real fortune still lay hidden somewhere back down that narrow, winding trail that descended into the huge chasm below.

How close they had come to finding it all! How terribly, terribly close! If they'd had just one more day. One more day and they'd have found that lost treasure and been richer than either had ever imagined.

A cold winter sun smiled weakly on Al's bare head. He had lost his hat in a desperate scramble up a trail so dangerous and narrow that it would intimidate even a mountain goat. He and Shorty Mike had somehow made the ascent with the Indians close on their heels. They could yet hear the echoing howls of rage, telling them that the Indians were mourning their dead.

"They'll come again and again," Al whispered to his badly shaken partner. "They'll keep coming until they overtake and kill us."

Shorty Mike nodded. "I'm almost out of ammunition. Emptied and then lost my six-gun before we even started up that trail."

Shorty shook his head. "We're too damn old for this shit!"

Al nodded and scrubbed his pointy, whiskered chin. "There's a fortune within two miles of us, Shorty. I can feel it in my bones! We were getting so close I could *smell* the gold!"

"What I smell is *blood*. Our own. I got hit by an arrow down there, Al. I got hit pretty bad."

Al twisted around suddenly to look at his partner, and that's when he saw the huge and spreading bloodstain on Shorty's woolen shirt.

"Jeezus!" Al whispered. "Why the hell didn't you say something before now!"

"What good would it have done?" Shorty grunted as he removed his jacket and unbuttoned his shirt. His skin was very white, and the wound was dark and pulsing a steady flow of blood.

Al's heart sank. The wound looked very bad. It was just to the left of Shorty's navel, and there was no way that it could not have pierced his gut.

"I'm a goner," Shorty gritted. "I'd be a goner even if you were a doctor."

"Don't talk like that!" Al snapped. "I seen men half blowed apart in the Civil War that lived, and they were ten times worse off than you."

"Bullshit," Shorty said, drawing a ragged breath, then buttoning up the shirt without even bothering to apply a bandage to stop the bleeding. "I'm finished, and there's only one thing left to do."

"What's that?" Al asked, the false bluster draining out of him, because both of them knew that Shorty was already a dead man.

"I'm going to stay right here and make sure that you put as many miles as you can between yourself and this death canyon."

Al shook his head. "I ain't just going to leave you here! Hell no! You know what those Indians will do to you."

"They can do whatever they like," Shorty said. "Because I'll save one bullet for myself. I won't be taken alive, you can bet on that much."

Al groaned. He looked up at the sun and decided that it was still a little before noon. But since the days of winter were short, only about six hours of light remained.

"Here," Shorty said. "Take this accursed Spanish gold and git!"

When Shorty's rough hand covered his own, Al almost broke down and wept.

"Take it!" Shorty said in a rough voice. "It sure as hell ain't going to do me any good where I'm going."

Al took the three pieces of gold, and his hand closed on that of his partner. "I'm sorry," he choked. "You never wanted to go down there in the first place. It was my idea. I'm the one that should have gotten killed."

"You got that much right," Shorty said, forcing a smile. "But sometimes the Lord calls His favorites first."

"And sometimes Satan does the same, needing some help," Al said with a wink, because this was a joke between them.

"You better—"

Both saw Indians appear just a hundred yards below on a ridge. Al and Shorty each fired and had the satisfaction of seeing two brown bodies hurl off the side of the trail and go spinning end over end, all the way to the rocks far, far below.

The other Indians disappeared, but their howls of rage were louder than ever.

Shorty grinned. "They'll think about coming around that bend pretty hard for another hour or two," he said. "I figure I can hold them back until dark."

"Jeezus," Al whispered, "I sure am sorry about the way this worked out."

"So am I. But sorry don't mean spit. So get those skinny old legs of yours churnin' south. If you're lucky enough to make it to Apache Junction, say hello and have a whiskey on me at the Geronimo Saloon and kiss that pretty daughter of yours."

Al sniffled and patted his old friend on the shoulder. "You want me to write your kinfolk in Missouri?"

"Naw. They always figured me a wandering fool. Only reason they ever gave me a minute's worth of their time was because they figured I might actually make a strike some day and be rich."

"Then I'll come back for your bones and bury 'em," Al said. "I'll do that."

"No!" Shorty lowered his voice. "Listen to me. After I kill myself, those howlin' sonsabitches will come racing up here and hack me to bits. Then they'll toss what's left of my old carcass over the side, and my bones will break on the rocks and scatter all the way down to the Colorado."

Al took a deep breath. He crabbed back from the rim and then stood up. His legs felt rubbery and he was shaking from his exertions, but he tried to look strong and resolute before his dying friend.

"I'll make it," he said. "And we'll toast you every time I belly up in the Geronimo."

"That'd be fine," Shorty said, his pain-stricken eyes never leaving the trail below. "So go on and take my canteen as well as your own. You'll need them both if you're to have any chance of making it out of this country."

Al did as he was told. "Good-bye, old friend," he said in a soft voice, kneeling and squeezing Shorty's boot. "I'm sorry we never got rich together. We would have been a pair, the both of us. We'd have been a couple of ring-tailed raccoons in old Frisco!"

"That we would have," Shorty said. "I just hope that you don't come back here for that Spanish gold."

"I *got* to! For the gold and to bury your bones."

"The hell with the gold and my bones!" Shorty cried. "Livin' is what's important. And if you come back, you'll end up the same as I have. So give me your word that you'll stay away from this cursed canyon."

Al shook his head slowly. "I can't do that."

"It's all I'm askin'!" Shorty cried. "It's my damn dyin' wish!"

Al pounded the earth with his bloodied fist. "I just can't do 'er, Shorty! I can't!"

"Shit!" Shorty swore. "All right then. Promise me you'll not come alone. That you'll bring some help."

"All right," Al said after a long pause. "I'll promise that much."

"Good. You're going to need at least a half-dozen fighting men. And I don't know how you'll get them down to the bottom. Saddle horses wouldn't make it— not even on the trail we used going down."

"Burros would, though," Al said. "We could bring five or six burros, and they'd pack all the supplies in and the gold out."

Shorty nodded with agreement. "How much do you really think is hidden down there?"

"Millions of dollars worth," Al said, his eyes going dreaming and distant. "I'll bet we'll find big chests of Spanish gold pieces."

"But how will you find where it's all cached?"

"I don't know," Al admitted. "If we'd had some time, I think we could have found it. We were real damn close, Shorty. So close that those Indians had to kill us."

"Yeah," Shorty said, "that's why they suddenly turned mean, ain't it."

"You bet it is," Al said. "They could see after we found those six pieces that we weren't about to go away without finding it all."

"We should never have showed 'em those Spanish pieces. That was our big mistake."

"It don't matter none now," Al said. "We can't worry about our past mistakes."

Shorty sniffled. "After today, I won't ever worry about anything again."

Al almost broke down and lost his composure, but he bit his lip until he tasted blood in his mouth to keep from crying.

Shorty expelled a long, ragged breath and said, "Git out of here before we both start blubberin'!"

Al had to wrench himself around and start off to the south. Leaving Shorty was the hardest thing he'd ever done in his life.

He walked steadily south, through the high desert, around the great stands of juniper and pinion pine, the towering outcroppings of rocks, under a dark, threatening sky.

Hour after hour he trudged on, lost in misery and sorrow. Twice he heard Shorty's old Winchester booming, and at sundown, he thought he heard the final shot.

Al wept like a baby. As dusk was falling, it began to rain, and the drops ran with his tears.

"It should have been me!" he kept muttering. "It should have been me!"

SEVEN

As the crow flew, it would have been less than a hundred miles to Apache Junction—a lot less. But since Al knew that he had to wind his way around a hundred obstacles, he figured his own trail would be slightly better than a hundred miles. Even worse was the realization that he'd be pursued by the hostile Grand Canyon Indians for at least the next two days.

"If I can make fifty miles, then they might give up," Al grunted as he struggled over a sage-covered rise. "Fifty miles and I've got a chance."

He had hurried all that first night and at dawn had curled up under a boulder and slept for several hours. Fortunately, he had a sack of jerky and some sourdough biscuits that were harder than rocks. His teeth were bad, so it hurt to chew, but somehow he'd choked the food down and found it gave him new strength.

Now, as he faced the second day of an estimated three—possibly even four—the clouds that had long been threatening a storm suddenly opened up and it began to pour.

Al wished mightily for his hat. The rain was cold and driven by a wind. Fortunately, he was wearing a damned good fleece-lined leather jacket, but by late afternoon, even that was pretty well soaked.

Every few minutes of every waking hour, he glanced over his shoulder, always expecting to see the Indians closing in on him. And when they did not and the rain began to come down in torrents, he began to think that he might even escape without a fight.

An hour before sundown, he turned his head back again almost automatically, a habit acquired after a thousand repetitions. Only this time, they were there. Six Indians. Not big men but small and wiry. They had bows and arrows, were dressed in the skins of deer, goat, and rabbit, and they were brown and determined. They were also closing in on him with amazing swiftness. And as he watched them close the distance to less than a mile, they appeared to the old prospector to move like wild things of the land.

"Oh no," he whispered, forcing himself into a stumbling run.

He ran on dead legs, legs without spring, that jarred his spine with every stride. He ran for his life, with the dim hope of reaching a jumble of rocks at the base of a cliff, where, like a cornered animal, he would make his last stand.

The legs began to fail him completely when he was about fifty yards away from the rocks. He felt his knees popping and then they began to wobble crazily, so that the next thing Al knew, he was spilling forward into the wet earth.

He looked back and the Indians were nocking their arrows, even though they were still out of range. It took all of his willpower not to throw his Winchester to his shoulder and drive them back, but Al knew that would be a fatal mistake. They would dive back into the earth if he did that. They would find cover behind the little bunches of sage and the small rocks. And then they would flank him, moving unseen like ghosts, until he was cut off from the sanctuary of his big boulders and trapped. And then they could lob their incredibly accurate little stone-tipped arrows in on him. The arrows would come in flurries, like the quail scattering before a hunter. At first, he might even elude them by ducking and rolling. But the arrows would come thicker and thicker until he could not move, and then he would feel them cutting through his coat and his flesh, bleeding his life away.

Al, his Winchester muddy and his heart choking in his throat, picked himself up and ran somehow. His legs were no longer a part of him. An arrow swooped past his right ear and bit into the mud, causing him to fall, but he scrambled up and staggered on.

The arrows were coming in all around him, and yet, miraculously, not a one struck him down before he threw himself into the rocks, fire in his lungs and ice in his heart.

They were so close! He punched the stock of his rifle to his shoulder and fired blindly. One shot. Two shots and then three!

The Indian charge wavered and one skidded to the earth, thrashing in the dirt and screeching with pain. The man's dying cries broke the resolve of his fellow tribesmen. The Indians stopped and unleashed more arrows, which shattered against the rocks. And then they fell back, dragging their dying friend.

Al rested his forehead against his leather sleeve. He fought for breath, gulping and wheezing, coughing and choking for air and courage.

"Come an' get me, you bastards!" he shouted, as lightning bolts stabbed into the high desert tableland and the earth shook with thunder. "Come on!"

A flight of fresh arrows answered his crazed challenge.

Al unleashed another bullet through the rain and ducked as the arrows broke against the leaking cliff behind him.

"Ha!" he screamed into the storm. "Now what the hell are you going to do!"

This time there was no answer, other than the fierce storm waging war against the Arizona sand.

"Bastards!" Al muttered. "You didn't want that Spanish fortune. You've *never* wanted it. You just want to keep it buried from us. Well, what good is it buried!"

His words were drowned by the rain and cracks of thunder that rolled like the cannon he had once heard at Shiloh and at the Battle of Bull Run.

What would they do? Would they come at him in the night? Al didn't know. Some men said that all Indians believed their spirits would be lost if they were killed in the darkness. If that were true, he could eat and sleep, maybe finding some strength in an old body bled of its last reserves.

But what if that were not true? What if the Indians used the cover of night to their obvious advantage? Surely they would! They could advance on him, be upon him in moments, and he would be helpless to stop them.

Al squinted the rain out of his eyes and watched the weak sunlight drain from the sky. He was sure that he would not live to see morning, but the question he now faced was this: Should he kill himself rather than risk being captured during a night attack?

He eased his back against the cliff, under a outcropping so that the rivulets of water did not pour directly upon him. Giving the question serious consideration, he gnawed on the cold hard biscuits and jerky.

At the end of an hour, the rain had eased up a little, and it was so dark all around him that he could not see his own hand. And if he could not see his hand, how would the canyon Indians see to capture him? The answer seemed rather obvious to Al Holland: The Indians could not see any better than he could, so they would not risk killing each other and they would not attack.

"They will come at first light," Al decided out loud. "They'll come like little black demons to have my gizzard and my scalp. But I will fight and kill as many as I can first. I owe that much to Shorty, so that is what I will do."

Al fell asleep under his rock. The sound of receding and distant thunder calmed rather than frightened him. He slept far better than he had expected, and when he awakened, it was to see a faint window of light on the eastern horizon. Just a crack that seemed to shimmer and finally, very gradually, to thicken like the eyeball of a man resisting wakefulness.

Al quickly gobbled a biscuit and washed it down with water from Shorty's canteen. He was sure that the Indians were moving in this very moment, even before they could spot him. And for that reason, he would have to shift some twenty or thirty yards along the base of the cliff. And then, when they howled and charged this place, he would kill some of them and see if he could not drive them away again. Like the day before.

He moved very cautiously, knowing that the lightning and the thunder would no longer mask sounds and that the Indians would be relying on their hearing far more than their sight. At the end of a quarter hour, he had covered a respectable distance. The eye in the early morning sky was almost open now, and through the broken storm clouds, he could see almost horizontal shafts of bright sunlight striking the soggy earth, lancing off the mountains.

God it was beautiful, this earth! Al breathed in the sharp aroma of sage and pine, he smelled the tang of wood and the deep heavy taste of earth, and he realized how very much he did not want to die, though he thought sure that he would within minutes.

His rifle was clenched in his hands, ready again. On his hip rested his trusty Colt, and he knew that he could use it very well.

Suddenly, he saw them again. They swarmed like hornets into the place he had first gone, and then they howled like maddened beasts to see that they had been tricked.

Al placed one of the larger Indians in his rifle sights and then he squeezed the trigger. The Indian was thrown back against the cliff. He did a little dance of death against the rocks while his tribesmen stood transfixed by the spectacle, until Al's Winchester brought another down.

Only three remained, and then they seemed to understand that now it was *they,* not the white man, who was at the disadvantage. Six to one were good odds, even given arrows against bullets. But three to one? Three to one was death.

"Come on!" Al screamed hoarsely as he jumped to his feet and shook the smoking rifle at them. "Come and get me! I *dare* you!"

One of the Indians launched himself forward with the glint of insane fury in his eyes. Al put the rifle to his shoulder and coolly shot the man in the leg. The Indian staggered and tried to nock his arrow. Al raised the rifle again, and the wounded man's nerve broke. He fell to the earth and covered his head.

"Go on!" Al shouted and gestured. "Go away! You've lost this time!"

The other two Indians had no trouble reading his meaning. They stood looking at him for almost a full minute, until they hurried to the wounded man's side and picked him up. One of the men cried out in anger and frustration, and Al could have shot all three down as they struggled to take their friend away. But he didn't. Instead, he waited until they were gone, and then he resumed walking toward Apache Junction.

EIGHT

Clint and Lucy were having a nice dinner of steak, potatoes, and French wine when a wild-eyed man burst into the restaurant, almost knocking the tray from a waiter's arms.

"Miss Holland!" he shouted as the room fell silent.

Lucy stood up quickly. "Over here!"

The man rushed across the room. "It's your father!" he blurted. "He's been found out on the desert! He's near death, Miss Holland!"

The forgotten glass of wine slipped from Lucy's hand and shattered on the floor as she turned with stricken eyes to Clint.

"Let's go," he said, taking Lucy's arm and guiding her to the door. "Has a doctor been sent for?"

"They're rounding up Doc Davis right now. Maybe you can ride out with him."

Clint nodded and headed for the doctor's office with Lucy. They could see a small gathering of men outside the doctor's office, and then the familiar pear-shaped form of the doctor emerged from his office, pulling on his coat.

"Doc!" Lucy cried. "We want to go with you!"

"You'll freeze without a coat."

Someone offered Lucy his coat, and then Clint was helping her up into the doctor's carriage. Two riders on nervous horses were ready, and when the doc gave a signal, the riders spurred their mounts north out of town.

"Hang on," Doc Davis warned. "I guess your father is only about five miles north of town. Some prospector found him dying."

"Oh my heavens, no!" Lucy cried, tears already in her eyes.

"Don't give up," Clint said. "A lot of men come back from what appears to be certain death. Your father is a tough old bird. He may just be worn down."

"They say he's babbling about Spanish gold," the doctor said. "I guess he's got few Spanish gold pieces on him, and everyone up north is pretty excited."

Lucy and Clint exchanged worried glances, and she said, "I don't give a damn about the Spanish gold. All I want is for my father to be all right."

"We'll see soon enough," the doctor promised, as his matched pair of sorrel geldings raced up the hard road, faintly illuminated by the moon and starlight.

It seemed to take forever to reach Al Holland's side, and they saw a collection of lanterns and torches long before they were there. When the doctor finally pulled his team to a standstill, Lucy and Clint were already bounding out of the wagon and racing to the old prospector's side.

"Make way for the man's daughter!" Clint shouted, helping Lucy fight her way to her father.

Al Holland's eyes were closed and his breathing was labored. He was as thin as a wraith and, to Clint's way of thinking, looked as if he had aged fifty years since last they'd shared a beer in the Geronimo. The old man's trousers were ripped out in the knees, and his shirt and coat were rags. He had the appearance of a man who had crawled and pulled himself out of the bowels of hell.

"Father!" Lucy cried, throwing herself at his side. "You can't die on me!"

Al roused himself enough to open his eyes. His arms lifted very heavily up and encircled his daughter. "I don't know if I'm going to make it this time," he choked. "But I got to talk to you in private about what I found."

"Later."

"No!" He hugged her closer, and everyone could see that he was whispering in her ear.

"Dammit, Al, let go of her and let me have a look at you!" Doc Davis bellowed. "You may not be so bad off as you think you are."

Al looked up at the portly doctor with his black medical bag.

"I'm dyin' for certain this time, Doc. Ain't no question about it."

"Let me decide who is dying and who is not dying," Davis grumped as he knelt by the prospector's side. "Give me better light!"

Several miners leaned forward with their lanterns, trying to offer the doctor a better view.

The doctor opened Al's shirt and placed his ear to the man's bony chest. "Breathe deep, in and out."

Al sucked in a lungful, then expelled it.

"Again."

Al did as he was told, only deeper this time, and it caused him to break into a mean-sounding cough. The doctor placed his hand on Al's forehead, then grabbed his wrist and checked his pulse. Finally, he pinched the prospector's cheek hard, and when Al yelped, the doctor seemed satisfied.

"You got pneumonia and you're starved. Other than that, I think you're just fine."

Lucy sniffled. "You mean he'll live?"

"I think so. He needs plenty of food and rest, but you can tell that just by looking at him. He's thinner than a winter-starved wolf. Let's get him back to your place, Miss Holland. In addition to being starved, he's also half-frozen."

Clint bent down and grabbed the old man under the arms, while another man grabbed Al by the legs. He seemed to weigh nothing at all. A couple of moments later, they had Lucy's father in the carriage and were heading back to Apache Junction.

"Say, Al!" a miner yelled. "Where did you get those pieces of Spanish gold!"

Clint was gazing right into the old man's shrunken face when Al shouted, "I may have pneumonia, but my brain ain't starved to death yet! You'll never know."

Some of the miners laughed, but Clint thought some of the others looked damned disappointed.

Al fought his pneumonia for two days, and Doc Davis said it was touch and go. "If he makes it to the end of the week, I think he's out of the woods."

"He'll make it," Lucy promised. "At least he will if I've got anything to say about it."

The doctor nodded. Lucy was a fine nurse, and she had not left her father's side for more than an hour since his arrival.

"I'll tell you this much," the doctor said. "Everyone in Apache Junction is rooting for him to pull through."

"He's well loved," Lucy said in agreement.

"Oh, he's that, all right, but even more important, they're all clamoring to know more about where he found that Spanish gold. I'll bet fifty men have asked me if your father has confided to me the whereabouts of his find. One of them was our mayor!"

"Doesn't surprise me," Clint said. "The man is as greedy for wealth as a hog for sweet corn. I'll just bet you he's even sent a couple of trackers to see if they can trace Al's backtrail to wherever he came from."

"Not much chance of that," Al said weakly. "It rained too damn much. I sure am sick about losing poor Shorty. I'm going to go back to bury him."

"Not for a month or so you're not," the doctor said. "Now, I don't care where you been or how much gold you found, my orders are the same: Stay in bed, fatten up, and do nothing but rest and recuperate."

"I'll have time to rest in the grave," Al grumped. "I've got a fortune in gold to discover, and I mean to do it just as soon as I can walk strong again."

The doctor took Lucy and Clint outside, where they could talk in private. "Your father greatly concerns me."

"Why?"

"He's not strong enough to keep up this life. It's a miracle that he was able to hike out of the desert and reach us. He almost didn't make it this time, Miss Holland. Somehow, you've got to convince him that his prospecting days are over."

"I can't," she said. "Prospecting is in his blood. It has been ever since I can remember. You might as well tell a bird not to fly."

Davis sighed. "All right. It's his funeral. I've told you what I know, and you and your father are the only ones who can make a difference now."

Lucy touched the doctor's sleeve. "Doc," she said, "we appreciate all that you've done for him. Really."

His brow lost its furrows. "Thanks," he said. "It's just

that it all seems such a waste of time if he's merely going to return to his old ways. Next time he won't make it to help."

"I know that. And I'll even plead with him to stay here with us, but I don't expect that he'll listen."

The doctor nodded to her and to Clint, then he headed out the door.

"So what's going to happen now?" Clint asked.

Lucy smiled. "We're going to go find that lost Spanish fortune, of course."

"Oh no!" Clint shook his head violently. "Your father said that the Indians killed his friend and almost lifted his own hair. No fortune is worth being scalped over, Lucy. I can tell you that much."

"My father disagrees, and so do I," she said. "And if you really won't go, then we'll just have to go without you."

Clint sighed with exasperation. "I need a drink," he said. "A stiff one."

"Tell the bartender it's on me and Father."

"Uh-uh," Clint said. "From now on, I'm buying my own."

Lucy's mouth turned down with disappointment. "I'm sorry to hear that. I guess that means you won't be going to the Grand Canyon with us."

Clint looked away, and then, without a word, he left the room. Lucy was as greedy as her father, though Clint had to force himself to admit the fact. Greed usually ended up getting people killed. Lucy was too young and pretty to die, but some folks were just bound and determined to get themselves killed by the lure of quick riches, no matter what you could tell them.

NINE

Mayor Wallace Boggs steepled his fingers and gazed thoughtfully across his desk at Marshal Timberman. "Is Charley Moffit on his way over here?"

"Yeah," Timberman said. "I told the old reprobate we were waiting. Told him to come in through your back office door and to make sure he wasn't seen by anyone."

"Do you really think he'll be able to learn where the Spanish gold is hidden?"

"What choice does he have?" the marshal asked. "I've got his partner in jail. I can trump up enough charges to send him to prison for at least five years. Charley will do anything for his partner. Those two are thicker than ants on wet candy."

The mayor nodded with satisfaction. "Have you heard anything more about where Holland found those Spanish gold pieces?"

Timberman shrugged his shoulders. "I heard it said he went to the Grand Canyon."

"Yeah, yeah," Boggs said impatiently. "I've been hearing the same thing. But that covers a lot of ground. We need something a whole lot more specific."

"Charley is good friends with Al Holland. You know those prospectors are real tight. He and Zeke will get a bottle of whiskey and get to see Al. Before the bottle is empty, Holland will be talking his head off. We'll know as much as he does by tonight."

"I hope so," Boggs said. "And I sure would like to see that Spanish fortune. We could both live like kings the rest of our lives with that kind of money."

"We'll find it," Timberman said, "and—"

His words were cut off in midsentence as the back door to the mayor's office opened quietly, to reveal an old man wearing bib overalls and a battered hat.

"Come on in and close the door!" Timberman growled.

Charley Moffit did as he was told. He was a short, bandy-legged man well up into his sixties. A shock of white hair as thin and fine as corn silk covered his head, and his eyes were pale and a little rheumy.

"Sit down!" Timberman ordered.

Charley sat, hat in his gnarled old hands, eyes fixed on the mayor's expensive rug.

Boggs cleared his throat to speak, but Timberman waved him to silence. "Mayor, if you don't mind, I'll handle this," he said, his eyes boring into the old man.

Timberman jabbed a finger at the prospector. "Charley, I got your friend Pete in my jail, and I'm going to see that he stays there a long damn time. No blankets, bad food, no company. And after he's rotted in that shivering jail for a good long while, I'll see that we come up with some charges that will get him sent to prison. Do you understand me?"

Charley raised his head for the first time and looked at the two men with eyes that burned with hatred. "Pete didn't do nothing but raise a little hell."

"He did enough," Timberman said. "So unless you want

him to go to prison, you're going to find out where those Spanish gold pieces came from."

Charley looked back down at the floor. "I told you already. They come from the Grand Canyon."

"We know that!" Boggs said angrily. "The question is, *where* in that big damn canyon! Now, Al and Zeke, they trust you. I'll pay for the whiskey, but I want answers."

"How do I know you'll let Pete go free, Marshal?"

"You don't. You'll just have to trust me on it."

Charley looked up. "I wouldn't trust either one of you farther than I could piss maple syrup."

The back of Ulysses Timberman's hand blurred, and Charley grunted with pain as his head snapped back. Timberman grabbed him by the front of the shirt and hauled him to his feet and began to shake the life out of him.

"Easy!" Boggs shouted. "You'll snap his neck if you keep shaking him that hard."

Timberman released the old man, shoving him backward so that he almost lost his balance and fell. "Don't you *ever* get smart-mouthed with me, you ragged, drunken old derelict!"

Charley raised his head. A trickle of blood flowed from a split lip. "If I was young again, I'd—"

"You wouldn't do any more than you're doin' now," Timberman said with contempt.

"Can I go?" Charley whispered, wiping the blood from his mouth with the back of his sleeve.

Boggs came to his feet and moved over to the old prospector. "The marshal plays a little too rough sometimes," he said, reaching into his pocket and pulling out a roll of greenbacks. "Here, take this and buy yourself some new clothes and . . . and whatever else it is you need. Maybe a bath and shave."

"Not before he finds out what we need to know!" Timberman said in anger. "Why, if he got together with Zeke and Al Holland all cleaned up and wearing new clothes, they'd know someone was putting him up to something."

Boggs nodded. He put all the money back into his pocket, except for five dollars. "Here," he said, "buy a bottle and find out what we need to know, then come back and I'll see that you get more."

"It's Pete that I want out of jail."

"That'll happen too," Boggs said, wrinkling his nose because the old man obviously had not bathed in weeks, perhaps even months.

When Charley Moffit left, he bought two bottles of cheap whiskey, sampled each of them generously, then went straight to find Zeke.

"Good to see you looking better," he said, pulling a bottle out of his coat. "Have a taste?"

"Damn right," Zeke said, taking the bottle and swilling it down. "Damn, that's bad whiskey!"

"Couldn't tell it by the way you drank it down," Charley said.

Zeke drank again, and when he cleared his throat he said, "I hear that they got old Pete in jail for disturbin' the peace."

"That's right. But he'll be out soon."

"Good," Zeke said. "That Ulysses Timberman is a mean sonofabitch. I wouldn't put anything past him."

"Neither would I," Charley said, not meeting Zeke's eyes. "I'm going over to share a bottle with Al. Wanna come along?"

"Why sure," Zeke said. "But this bottle will be mostly empty by the time we get to Al."

Charley patted his coat pocket. "I got another where that come from."

"Hot damn!" Zeke said.

Ten minutes later, Zeke and Charley were sitting on the floor, looking up at Al Holland, who was taking his first long taste of whiskey.

"Jeezus, that's bad stuff!" Al complained, his face contorting into a grimace. "Why don't you get my daughter to sell you some of our whiskey? The cheapest we pour is a whole lot better than this panther piss!"

"You're getting mighty finicky in your old age," Charley said with a sad smile.

Charley would have really enjoyed himself during the next couple of hours, if not for the fact that he knew he was expected to gain information about the location of the Spanish gold. And if he failed to do that, his partner was going to rot in the Apache Junction jail, and Pete's health was none too strong anyway.

Charley waited nearly two hours, and by then both bottles were emptied and they'd half finished off a third.

"I was thinkin'," he began, trying to look into Al Holland's thin face, "that maybe you and Zeke and I could go hunting that Spanish gold. You're going to need some experienced men."

Al's smile faded. "I dunno," he said. "My daughter and the Gunsmith are coming along."

This news was a big surprise. Charley frowned. "Well, you're still going to need experienced mining men to find that gold. And you'll need extra guns to keep the Indians from lifting your scalps."

Al shrugged. "The Gunsmith is worth half a dozen normal gunmen."

"At least," drawled Zeke, who was the drunkest of the three.

"I still think you'll need Zeke and me to help you find that hidden gold."

Al furrowed his brow. "I dunno," he said thoughtfully.

"It's a long, hard trail, and I'm not sure that you and Zeke are up to it."

Zeke roused up enough to bristle. "Well, the hell with that! Albert Holland, I can keep up with you any damn time or place."

"So can I," Charley said. "Even drunk."

"It's dangerous," Al said quietly. "I been trying to talk my daughter out of going down in that canyon, but she won't listen. It's just dangerous as anything. The trail leadin' up and down that canyon wall will put the fear of the Lord in your heart. You'll think for sure that you'll never reach the bottom where the Colorado flows, and if you do, you'll be sure you'll never get out alive."

"I'll take my chances for a little of that Spanish gold," Charley said.

"I feel the same way," Zeke announced. "The Juniper Mountains will still be waiting when I get back."

"All right then," Al said, "you can both come along. But that's all."

Charley frowned. "My partner, Pete—he'd want to go too, once I get him sobered up and out of the marshal's jail."

Al sighed. "What the hell. There's a fortune down in that canyon. All right. Pete's in. But no more."

Charley wrung his hands together. "I do have one little problem, friends. I'm afraid that the mayor and the marshal are the ones that paid for the whiskey we drunk. You see, they're expecting me to come tell them where the Spanish gold is to be found, so they can get it first."

Zeke's jaw dropped with amazement. "You mean to tell me they sent you over here to trick old Al!"

"That's right. Timberman said he'd keep Pete in his jail forever if I didn't cooperate."

Al shook his head. "Don't fret none over it, Charley.

I'll even draw you a map leadin' to the canyon that will take them on a wild goose chase."

For the first time, Charley's mouth widened into a genuine smile. "Damn, I'd appreciate that! I sure am glad you ain't angry at me for what I had to do."

Al waved his hand to dismiss the matter. "You got to get Pete out of jail, don't you? So now the last laugh is on the marshal and Boggs! Think of what a pair of fools they'll look like to everyone when they come straggling back to Apache Junction a few weeks from now, with worn-out horses and empty pockets!"

All three old prospectors laughed uproariously, and Al rummaged around Lucy's room until he found a paper and pencil.

"Let's see," he began. "First I'll draw the Grand Canyon, and then I'll draw a trail leading down square into the Indians' camp. That ought to fix things real good for our greedy friends."

Zeke cackled, and Charley grinned from ear to ear. Sure as hell, he thought, things were going to work out just fine after all.

TEN

Charley knocked softly on the mayor's back door. He was still a little drunk, but he, Zeke, and Al Holland had gone over what he was to tell these scheming bastards a good half dozen times, so Charley figured he would be all right.

"Come on in!" Timberman said, opening the door and grabbing Charley to pull him roughly inside.

"Keep your hands off me!" Charley snarled.

Timberman's fists clenched, but Charley stood his ground until the mayor's voice cut sharply between them.

"Ulysses, leave him alone, dammit!"

The marshal's eyes were hot. "When this is over, you and your partner ought to think about moving to another town."

"Maybe we won't have to," Charley said, raising his chin. "If the Grand Canyon Indians kill you, maybe we'll all be better off around Apache Junction."

Timberman would have struck him, but the mayor was already pushing between them. "I said, leave the old man be!"

Timberman backed away. "Ask him what he's got."

Boggs turned to Charley. "Did you find out what we want to know?"

"I did."

"Let's hear it."

"Not until he lets Pete out of jail."

"No!" Timberman said. "He's just trying to double-cross us."

Charley stood his ground. "If I tried to do that, you'd know and arrest us both. We're in no shape to run."

Boggs studied the old man, then turned to the marshal. "He's right. You could just arrest them both."

The mayor had a fancy liquor cabinet, and he went over to it and filled two glasses—one for himself and one for Charley. "Marshal, why don't you go release Pete from jail."

"I want to see him," Charley said. "I'll have to see him free before I tell you where that Spanish gold is waitin'."

Timberman started to protest, but the mayor cut his objection off short. "Do as he says, Marshal. We've wasted enough time."

Timberman went stomping out the back door.

"He's a real hothead," Boggs said, sipping on his whiskey. "But he's loyal and he has guts. I sure hope that you aren't trying any tricks on us, Charley. If you were, I just don't think I could keep the marshal from killing you both."

Charley swallowed nervously. "I guess I know that," he said, tossing down his whiskey and holding out his glass for a refill.

Ten minutes later, the marshal appeared with Pete. He shoved the old prospector up the alley and came inside.

"Well, you saw him," Timberman growled. "Now start talking."

Charley knew he'd played it out as far as he could.

Looking defeated, he pulled the map that Al Holland had just drawn out of his pocket. "Here it is," he said, handing the map to Boggs.

"Al drew this?"

"Yep."

"Why?"

"Because I got him drunk and he needs some friends to go with him. He told me that if something happened to him out on the trail or down in that canyon, I was to use this map to find the Spanish fortune, then make sure that his daughter got the biggest share."

Timberman and Boggs exchanged glances and then smoothed the map out on a table. They studied it intently for several minutes, then the mayor said, "Why, this doesn't tell us anything!"

"Sure it does," Charley said, leaning over the map, and he began to explain how easy it would be to follow. When he was finished, he asked, "Can I go now?"

"Hell no!" Timberman said. "I think this map is bullshit! I think you've just drawn it up to send us off in the wrong direction."

Charley's belly went hard with fear and he expected to die, but the mayor said, "I don't. I think this map is accurate."

"What!" Timberman roared in amazement. "You can't be serious!"

"I *am* serious," Boggs said. Before Timberman could erupt in anger, Boggs pulled a wad of greenbacks out of his pocket and shoved them into Charley's hand. "Thanks. Now you'd better get out of here."

Charley could have wept with relief. It had worked! Nodding his head up and down and not daring to look at the marshal, who appeared ready to explode, he jumped for the door and was gone in a flash.

Timberman was fit to be tied. "Did you really believe that lyin' old bastard?"

The mayor filled their glasses and reclined in his leather office chair. "Nope."

"Then why'd you make me let Pete out of jail!"

"Because," Boggs said, "I want Charley, Al, and the rest of them to *think* we took their bait."

Boggs wadded up the map that Charley had given him and tossed it into his wastebasket. "As for this, it isn't worth a thing. We'll just let them believe we swallowed their story, and then we'll follow them right to the Grand Canyon. After they've found the gold and fought off the Indians, then we'll step in and take us a Spanish fortune."

Timberman visibly relaxed. "I like your thinking. But we'll need some pretty good men. There's no telling how many Indians are in that canyon."

Boggs wholeheartedly agreed. "That'll be your department. Hire at least a dozen, and make sure they'll stand and fight when the going gets rough."

"Can I tell them about the Spanish gold?"

"Not until after Holland and the rest have departed."

Timberman headed for the door, then stopped and chuckled.

"What's so funny?" Boggs asked.

"I was just thinking about the Gunsmith. Can you imagine this? He's going out with a woman and three, maybe four old men! Nothing but old men and a woman!"

Timberman laughed out loud, but not Boggs. "Listen," the mayor said, "I want that woman for myself. And as for the 'old men,' don't underestimate any of them."

"Are you serious?"

"Damn right I am," Boggs said. "They may be old and drink too much whiskey, but they'll be sober on the trail to the Grand Canyon, and I'll just bet all of them can shoot the balls off a bumblebee."

Timberman's smile died on his lips. "Yeah," he conceded, "you're probably right."

"You bet I am. And as for the Gunsmith, you know he's going to be a heller in a gunfight."

"I can take him."

Boggs snorted with derision. "Don't be stupid! A man like that has gunned down too many to be taken lightly. And why risk your own life so foolishly? The thing to do is to back-shoot him. Take no risks. Remember, we stand to be richer than kings if we find that hidden Spanish treasure."

"You're already rich," Timberman said.

"No one is *ever* rich enough," Boggs said. "Besides, most of my wealth is in property, and to be honest, I'd like to shake the dust of this miserable town and head for greener pastures."

Timberman's didn't understand that, but he believed it. Boggs was a strange man and a complicated one. He seemed to have everything—and yet nothing that gave him any real joy. He was secretly in love with Lucy Holland, a woman who openly despised him; and now he'd just revealed he did not like living in Apache Junction, even as its richest citizen and its mayor.

That did not make one bit of sense to Timberman. Not one bit of sense at all.

Later that afternoon, a lot of things did not make much sense to the Gunsmith, either. "I just don't understand why they'd use you to try and trick Al into learning where to find that Spanish treasure," he said.

Al scratched his head. "Seems obvious to me that they'd like to beat us there."

"I don't know," Clint said dubiously. "Put yourself in the place of Boggs and Timberman. Why would you want to leave with us coming up your backtrail? You'd be the ones that would have to meet the Indians head-on and try to defeat them. You'd take all the risks and then, sooner or later, you'd have to face us from behind."

Al frowned. "Are you saying that you don't believe they'll follow the fake map I drew?"

"That's right. I think they might make a big show of leaving first, but then they'll double back and let us get ahead of them, and they'll trail us right to the Grand Canyon and let us take all the risks."

"So what do we do?" Lucy asked.

"We go as planned, only we cover our trail and lose them. They'll get confused and have to try and follow your map, since they have no other directions. If they do that, then we strike out for the real location of the lost treasure."

Clint looked at the four old men and Lucy. "Is everybody agreeable to that plan?"

They all nodded.

"Good!" Clint shook hands all around. "I see no reason why we can't leave the day after tomorrow."

"Why not tomorrow?" Al asked.

"Because Doc Davis would have a fit over us taking you out so soon."

Al frowned. "To hell with him! He'll have a fit anyway. I say we go tomorrow."

"Suits me," Clint said.

"Me too," Lucy said.

Charley grinned. "Then let's do it!"

That agreed, each opened a bottle of Lucy's best champagne and they raised them in a toast.

"To Spanish gold!" Lucy cried.

"To Spanish gold!" they all echoed.

Clint and Lucy drank with the old men for several minutes and then, almost as if by a silent signal, they excused
themselves and headed for Clint's hotel, where they could
spend some time together making love in a warm, soft
feather bed.

"It's going to be a good long while until we can do
it together in comfort again," Clint said as they hurried
across the street to his hotel.

"I know," Lucy said, hugging his waist. "But comfort-
able or not and no matter how long and dangerous the trail
we're about to undertake, I'll bet we find a way to do it
anyhow."

Clint laughed and squeezed Lucy tight, even as his mind
worried over what might lie ahead and how much of a
danger he'd have to face in order to bring Lucy and the
old men back to Apache Junction alive.

"My dear," he said, "that's a bet I wouldn't take for
anything."

ELEVEN

It was cold, miserable, and rainy the first night out of Apache Junction, as Clint led Lucy and the four grizzled old prospectors.

"We're just lucky that it hasn't turned to sleet or snow," he yelled into the rain. "Best thing about all this rain is that it will wash out our tracks."

Lucy, wrapped in a slicker and with water running off the brim of her hat, could only nod and try to keep her teeth from chattering. She kept looking over at her father, who was trudging through the falling rain, leading his mule. The doctor was furious that they'd left in a winter storm, but everyone had agreed that it was a blessing if it would throw the mayor's crowd off their backtrail.

"Father!" Lucy yelled. "Will you please ride my horse and let me walk!"

Old Al Holland shook his head. He would rather die than ride while his prospecting buddies trudged through the rain, leading their sturdy little pack mules.

The rain did not let up until dawn, and then the sun broke through the clouds and there was a brilliant rainbow that stretched hundreds of miles across the horizon.

"It's a sign from the Lord!" Charley called. "He's telling

us that we will finally find that pot of gold at the end of his rainbow."

"Aw, horseshit," Pete grumped. "You're always seeing signs in things, and none of them ever mean anything."

"The hell you say!" Charley swore, clenching his fists and glaring at his partner.

Al turned on Charley. "For crying out loud!" he complained. "We're off to face hostile Indians, a canyon that no sane man would ever go down into, and we'll probably all get ourselves killed before we get rich. So why don't you and your partner quit feudin' and get along together!"

"He's right," Clint said, squinting into the northern horizon. "We're facing long odds any way you look at it. The last thing we need is to quarrel among ourselves."

Charley and Pete shot each other hard glances, and Clint found himself wondering if this entire expedition wasn't going to be snake-bitten right from the start. He sure hadn't wanted to come along, but seeing as how there was little doubt that his gun would be needed if Lucy, her father, and these cantankerous old prospectors were to survive, he hadn't felt there was much of a choice.

As if reading his mind, Lucy leaned out of her saddle a little and said, "You just wait and see if we don't come back richer than an Egyptian king."

"All I want is to see us come back alive," Clint said. "And since you already own the finest saloon, dancehall, and hotel in northern Arizona, I sure can't understand why you're taking a risk like this."

"Because she's my daughter!" Al Holland interrupted. "Hell, Clint, you of all men ought to understand why adventure and the chance to win a fortune stirs the blood."

"Just surviving on the western frontier is adventure

enough," Clint said. "I've killed too damn many men whose only sin was that they were greedy and in search of adventure at someone else's expense."

"Whose expense are we doin' this at?" Charley demanded.

Clint would have preferred to change the subject, but since they were all staring at him, he decided to speak his mind. "Well, so far, at the expense of about three Indians' and Shorty Mike's lives," he said. "And I'll tell you another thing: Some of us aren't going to make it back to Apache Junction."

Clint was cold, wet, and in an ill humor. "It's one thing to take risks to save someone's hide or do something to right an injustice. But to take risks just for riches, well, I don't put that in the same damn category."

Lucy didn't say anything and neither did the four old miners, so Clint just rode along, trying to keep his teeth from chattering. Maybe he'd made them all angry, but he didn't care. If they did find the Spanish gold, they'd have to kill some Indians to bring it out of the Grand Canyon, and, unless Clint was mighty surprised, they would wind up fighting Wallace Boggs, Ulysses Timberman, and a whole mess of others. Wealth attracted the worst kind of men; it attracted them like carrion did flies.

Late that afternoon, Clint called for a rest stop. The prospectors were plenty glad, and when Clint tied Duke to a pinion pine and started to hike up a rock-strewn hillock, Lucy hurried to join him.

"Why are you so angry?"

"Because I think we're going to lose some damn nice old men," Clint said, not even slowing down as he attacked the hill.

Lucy had to work hard to keep up with him. "Don't you think that they know the risks? Don't you think that all of us ought to have the right to decide for ourselves if the chance of getting rich is worth the gamble?"

Clint didn't answer until he came to the crest of the hill and had carefully studied his backtrail and was confident that they weren't being closely followed.

"Yes," he said at last, "I think everyone ought to have the right to choose their own risks. It's just that I'm not sure that those men really understand the kind of predicament we're putting ourselves in. Most certainly Boggs and Timberman are somewhere behind us, and they'll have plenty of gunmen. And furthermore, I don't much like the idea of killing off a bunch of Indians who are simply trying to protect their homeland from a horde of treasure seekers."

Lucy's cheeks colored with anger. "If you're so dead set against coming, then turn back right now. We don't need you."

"The hell you don't," Clint said. "If I leave, you won't ever see Apache Junction again."

Lucy turned and stomped down the hill to rejoin her father and the rest of the prospectors. Clint could see by the way she moved that she was furious at him, but he didn't much care. He'd done everything he could to talk them out of this venture; now the best he could do was to keep them stirred up and on their guard, because sure as the sun was going to set in the west and rise in the east, there was big trouble both ahead and behind them.

For the next two days, they traveled steadily northwest, all of them quiet and determined to reach the southern rim of the Grand Canyon by the end of that third day.

Once they saw a large band of wild horses led by a magnificent pinto stallion. The stallion trumpeted a challenge at Duke and the big gelding whinnied back, pawing and stamping his feet.

"Never mind him," Clint said as the stallion tossed its head in the wind. "And as for his mares, well, I'm afraid the best you can do is just admire."

Duke nickered softly. He acted as if he were a stallion himself, and that made Clint smile.

"Do you think it's that funny?" Lucy asked.

"In a way," he said. "I mean, suppose that he were free and he challenged and whipped the pinto—which he's sure big and strong enough to do. What then?"

Lucy tried to hide her own smile. "I see your point. But lust is often more satisfying than reality."

"Tell that to the horse," Clint snorted, and he spurred out ahead to chase the stallion and his mares, thundering off into the brush.

It was almost sundown when they came to the southern rim of the canyon. None but Al had ever gazed into that awesome void before, and with the dying rays of sunlight glinting off the fantastic rock monuments and spires, it was a sight they knew they would never again match.

"It's incredibly beautiful!" Lucy breathed. "My father has described it over and over, but words could not begin to tell you what it really looks like."

Clint fully agreed. "It makes this all worthwhile. Spanish gold or no Spanish gold. It's something not to be missed."

Even their hearty little burros were impressed. With their legs braced wide apart, they stuck their necks out over the rim and snorted with a mixture of fear and wonder at the sight of the great canyon, with its brilliant colors and shining river far, far below.

"We're really going to get to the bottom of that?" Charley asked.

"Yeah," Al said. "When the Indians were chasing me

and Shorty, we came up a game trail so narrow that even these sure-footed burros couldn't climb it. But we'd gone down a little wider trail about six or seven miles to the west of here. We can reach it early tomorrow and start down right away."

Al suddenly stiffened. "There!" he said in a strangled voice. "You see him!"

"Who?"

"Shorty."

Even Clint paled a little as he followed the old prospector's pointed finger down a trail that looked impossibly narrow. And just about ten feet below the trail, hanging suspended by his coat and pincushioned by at least twenty arrows, was the body of a man.

"Oh my God!" Lucy cried, covering her eyes.

Al wiped his eyes of tears. "I've got to try and reach him."

"Wait!" Clint went to his horse. "I'll help you with my rope."

Al nodded, and together, they started down the little game trail that was not more than two feet wide in any one spot and often less than eighteen inches.

If Al was as scared as Clint while he slowly edged down the trail, he didn't show it. But Clint, quite honestly, was damn near terrified. He would rather have faced a dozen gunmen or rampaging Indians than inch down that narrow trail, where one slight misstep would send him tumbling hundreds of feet to the rocks below.

"What are we going to do now?" Al asked, stopping just above the suspended body.

"I dunno," Clint admitted, pressing his back to the hard cliff and peering over the side at the body. "I guess we'll try and lasso and then drag him up."

"Yeah," Al said. "I guess that's all we can do."

Clint had never roped downward, and it took him several heart-pounding attempts before he managed to get his loop around the body. But then, he was stumped. If they tried to drag Shorty's body up, it would very likely pull them over the edge.

"You can't do it!" Charley shouted from above. "If you try, you'll both go over the side!"

Charley's opinion was loudly echoed by the others. Especially Lucy. "Father, let it go!" she cried. "Shorty wouldn't have wanted you to die over his corpse!"

Clint took a deep, steadying breath and looked sideways at the old prospector, who was caught in an agonizing dilemma. "She's right, Al. Your partner gave his life to save yours. Don't throw it away now."

"Okay," Al said, as the sun was dying. "But I won't leave his body dangling in the air for the buzzards to strike and tear at. Let's pull him off that branch and then drop him. I'll find him down below and bury whatever is left."

Clint understood. He nodded, and he and Al pulled the body up several feet, swung it sideways, and then released the rope.

Clint saw the body spin crazily down into the canyon to strike a rock, bounce, and roll into some brush. "Al, I'm real sorry about this. If there had been some way—"

"Forget it!" Al snapped. "We would have lost our balance and gone over with him. I'll take care of Shorty when we reach the bottom tomorrow evening."

Clint said nothing as he inched his way back up the steep, narrow trail. And even though the air was cold, his body was drenched in sweat by the time he climbed back over the lip of the canyon.

Hell, he thought, as he went to gather firewood and take the chill from his body, I haven't even gone down there yet, and already the place has me spooked.

TWELVE

Mayor Wallace Boggs had never been so miserable in his entire life. Despite the best rain slicker that money could buy, he was soaked to the skin, chilled to the bone, and madder than hell.

"You mean to say that we've completely lost their tracks!"

"That's right," Marshal Timberman snarled. "What the hell do you expect in this weather! The way it rained the last few days, we're lucky we haven't drowned, let alone lost the tracks."

Boggs roughly jerked his horse to a standstill and piled off into the mud. "Goddamn cinch is loose again," he complained.

No one said anything. Not Ulysses Timberman, who'd already had a bellyfull of the mayor's constant bitching, and not the dozen hired gunmen, who saw images of Spanish gold dancing before their bloodshot eyes.

"So what are we going to do now!" Boggs demanded. "We got nothing to follow to the Grand Canyon."

Timberman glanced up at the sky, silently cursing the dark, threatening clouds. The hell with it, he thought as he signaled the other riders to dismount. They had not dried out since leaving Apache Junction almost three days before. Timberman was not a fastidious man, but he could literally feel his feet moldering away in his soggy socks.

"Let's make camp under these trees," he said, leading his horse up to the nearest big pine and tying it securely, before he loosened his cinch and yanked his saddle from the back of his steaming mount.

"Well I just tightened my cinch!" Boggs swore.

"So untighten it," Timberman growled. "There's a little dry grass here, and the horses need to eat and rest as bad as we do."

"How far to the rim of the canyon?" Boggs asked, for about the fiftieth time since they'd left Apache Junction.

"Maybe twenty miles," Timberman said. "Twenty-five. No more."

Boggs waddled over to tie his own horse next to that of Timberman's, but their mounts squealed and snapped at each other, as irritable as the men.

"Tie that animal of yours off by itself," Timberman said. "He's lookin' for a fight. Last thing we need is for one of 'em to kick and cripple another and leave one of us afoot."

Boggs did not like to follow anyone's orders, but when he opened his mouth, he noted Timberman's menacing expression and decided that this was not the time or the place to make authority an issue. And to be fair about it, this kind of nasty business was the thing that Timberman was paid to do.

Boggs relocated, then uncinched his horse, dumped his wet saddle on the ground, and went over to stand under a tree while his men made camp.

"I still think we should have ridden on until dark," Boggs complained, though he was secretly relieved to be stopping early for the night.

"We'll cut across their tracks tomorrow or the next day," one of the gunmen grunted.

"How do you know that?" Boggs demanded. "We might have wandered fifty miles off their trail. How are we even going to know which way to search after we reach the canyon?"

Timberman struck a match, which sputtered in the damp air and died. He struck another, touching it to a handful of dry pine needles he'd gathered under the trees. The needles smoked, then flamed sullenly. Timberman motioned for some kindling, which was immediately provided. In just a few minutes, he had a good fire, though one very smoky.

"I asked you a question," Boggs said, furious at being ignored by the taciturn marshal. "I want to know how you'll decide in which direction to ride along the canyon's rim."

Timberman looked up at the man. Boggs outweighed and maybe even outmuscled him, but the mayor wasn't a veteran fighter, and the marshal knew that all it would take was one good hit to the man's crotch and Boggs would be completely helpless. And it would be so easy right now.

"Listen," Timberman said, exercising the very last vestige of his patience, "you and I will get along a whole lot better if you just relax and let me do the work I do best. I don't try to tell you how to run Apache Junction; don't try to tell me how to track down men. Okay?"

"I asked you a simple question," Boggs said, aware that all conversation had stopped and everyone was staring at him and Timberman, half expecting a showdown. "I think I deserve an answer."

"All right!" The marshal came to his feet, a stick in his hand and murder in his eyes. "*If* we haven't cut their sign by the time we reach the rim, then we'll just have to split up and ride in both directions along the rim until we do cut across their sign."

"Split our forces?" Boggs shook his head. "Then we'd number about the same as the men we're chasing! It doesn't make sense to lower our odds that way, Marshal."

"It does to me," Timberman snapped. "Because the way I see it, we shouldn't even be going down into that canyon. What we do is locate the Gunsmith and the others, then we camp out on the rim and just wait and let them do the dangerous work down below."

Boggs had started to object, but now he saw that the marshal was right. "Sure," he whispered. "Why should we risk our lives unless we have to? Let the Gunsmith and those old bastards fight the Indians. We'll stay on top, and we'll take any survivors and any gold they retrieve."

"Exactly." Timberman relaxed. "The only problem we have is if the Gunsmith should spot us up on top and try to escape. That, or if he and his party get butchered by the Indians. In that case, I'm not sure whether I'd be willing to go down into that canyon."

"Not even for a fortune?"

"We don't know for sure that there's any fortune," Timberman spat. "Maybe hundreds of years ago some Spaniards just gave the Indians a handful of gold coins to buy peace. Hell, maybe the only Spanish gold down there was what old Holland brought back."

"What a depressing thought!" Boggs said. "I mean, it wasn't cheap hiring all these men. They'll get paid even if we don't find treasure."

"You can afford 'em," the marshal said. "Me, I'll probably lose my job after Judge Stallings writes a few letters to his cronies. I'm banking on some gold, and so are these men."

The gunmen around them nodded in agreement. Boggs expelled a deep breath and rubbed his hands over the flames. "I think someone ought to start cooking," he grumped. "I'm hungry enough to eat a horse."

Timberman piled more wood on the fire. He heard the growl of distant thunder and wished that he could have left the mayor back in Apache Junction. The man was like a saddle sore that galled at every stride. He was always complaining, always trying to tell a man how to do his job.

Timberman jabbed a stick at the fire. Well, one thing that Boggs didn't know, and that was that if they found Spanish gold and got it out of the canyon, he and some of his men would never live to spend it. With a fortune at stake, the fool mayor seemed to have no idea at all that the game they played would be strictly a matter of the survival of the fittest.

The next morning, Timberman roused his men before dawn and they were in the saddle at first light, riding at a steady, mile-eating trot. Everyone's eyes were on the ground, searching for fresh tracks, but they saw not a one all morning, and when they reached the Grand Canyon and beheld its grandeur and immensity, they fell into silence.

"All right," Boggs said after a few minutes, "I'm not paying you men to sightsee. Let's figure out who is riding with who and get moving."

Timberman nodded. "I'll take one group, Mayor; you take the other."

Boggs was trapped and he knew it. Timberman was the best tracker and shot among them and the most dangerous fighter. It would have been best to stay with him, but Boggs knew he could not do that without losing face.

"All right," he said, picking his men. "Let's go. We'll

ride to the west; Timberman, you and your group go to the east."

"Okay."

Timberman and his group started to ride off, but Boggs shouted, "Well wait a damn minute! How we going to know when one or the other of us cuts across the Gunsmith's tracks!"

"Beats the hell out of me," Timberman said. "I guess if either one of us rides two or three days and still doesn't see anything, they can pretty well figure that they ought to turn around."

Boggs shook his head. "This just doesn't feel right to me. There ought to be a better arrangement."

"But there isn't," the marshal said. "Cause you see, out in this country, nothing ever works like a man intends. So you just have to take each day, each mile, and each damn problem as it comes and be ready. One of us might even run into hostile Indians out here. There are a hell of a lot of them besides the ones that live down in the canyon."

Boggs swallowed. "First I've heard of it."

Timberman damn near laughed out loud at the deep worry that had crept into the mayor's eyes. Instead, he shrugged his shoulders and said, "You got good fighting men with you, Boggs. Just listen to what they say if you get into a scrape, and if you don't catch a stray bullet or arrow, you'll do just fine."

One of the men snickered, but Wallace Boggs didn't see any humor in the situation at all. In fact, he had the distinct impression that he had somehow been outwitted by the marshal.

"Maybe I'll ride east instead of west," he said defensively.

"Suit yourself," Timberman said with apparent indifference. "The chances of cutting the Gunsmith's tracks are about the same in either direction."

"All right then," Boggs said. "I'll go east."

"Fine." Timberman motioned his men that it was time to leave, and when he rode away, Wallace Boggs was thinking that he should have taken his men west, like he'd first thought to do.

THIRTEEN

At sunrise the next morning, it was obvious that Pete was exhausted and feeling weak. Clint knelt on his heels and said, "We need a volunteer to remain up here on the rim to watch for trouble and take care of Miss Lucy's horse and my own. I'd appreciate it if you'd be the man for that job."

Pete cocked an eye at him. "And miss the chance to see that Spanish gold! No thanks."

"I know it's the raw end of the deal," Clint said. "You'd be our eyes and ears up here. Timberman, Boggs, and the rest of that crowd may come along before we can get back out, and then you'd be in a hell of a fix."

Pete sniffled. "That big gelding of yours let me ride him?"

"Yeah, he would," Clint said.

"Well then, between him and Miss Lucy's horse, nobody would catch me if I decided to run."

"Like I said," Clint drawled, "it's the most dangerous job any of us could have, staying up here. But I sure think you're the best man for it, Pete."

If Pete knew that he was being conned, he didn't let on. Instead, he sort of puffed up with self-importance. "Well, maybe I will stay then."

"Would you!" Clint beamed. "Boy, that sure would be a load off our minds to have you up here watching out for us, while we're down below."

"I'll do it," Pete said.

Clint pumped the old man's hand. "We're all much obliged. And don't worry—we'll do our best to see that we all get rich."

"You do that."

"If everything goes well," Clint said to the weary prospector, "we could find the Spanish treasure, load it on the burros, and be back up here to join you by tomorrow at sundown."

Pete was reclined on the ground, back propped up against a rock, face warmed by the sun. "Nothin' ever goes *that* slick, Gunsmith. You know that as well as I do. Most likely, you'll come scramblin' back up that awful cliff with nothing more than your life."

"If that's what you think," Clint said, "why'd you even come along?"

"For the fun of it," Pete said without hesitation. "And because somewhere out there, Marshal Timberman and that sonofabitchin' mayor are trying to beat us to the Spanish gold. After the way Timberman roughed me up in his jail, I sure couldn't sit by and allow the man to get rich now, could I?"

"I guess not," Clint conceded.

Lucy came over to say good-bye. "We've left you plenty of food and water, Pete. All you have to do is rest up and keep a lookout for trouble."

"Yeah, I know," the prospector said. "And if I see Timberman or Boggs, I'm going to shoot their eyes out, then climb on that big black gelding and get out of here before they can catch me."

"Good," Clint said. "Duke isn't hard to ride, and he's

fast as well as strong. Just don't use him too hard, and he'll keep you ahead of trouble."

"I can see that," Pete said, looking toward the grazing horse with admiration. "But the truth of the matter is that I hope that I'm sittin' right here when you come struggling up out of that canyon and it's all those burros can do to tote up the rest of that Spanish gold."

"That would be nice," Clint said, patting the weary old man on his shoulder. "Just rest up and we'll do our best."

When they were ready to make the descent to the Colorado, Charley went over to his old friend to say good-bye. He'd prospected for more than twenty years with Pete, and he loved his partner like a brother.

"You always did get the easy part of things," he growled at his exhausted friend. "Beats me how you did it again this time."

"Just lucky, I guess." Pete reached up to extend his hand. "Charley, you take it easy and watch your scalp down below. Al says them Canyon Indians are pretty good shots with their bows and arrows."

"Hell, my hair is so thin it's not worth their bother! It's you that should keep an eye out for trouble. The Gunsmith figures that nobody could have followed our washed-out tracks to this place, but Timberman is no dummy. He'll find us—and maybe before we get back."

"If he does, I'll put a bullet in him," Pete vowed.

"No, your eyes ain't sharp like they used to be," Charley said. "So if you see Timberman or his boys, I want you to just climb on the Gunsmith's horse and skedaddle. You understand?"

"Yeah," Pete said quietly. "Right after I kill that marshal."

Charley shook his head. "Old Al already lost Shorty. I don't want to lose my partner, too."

"If you do, you and Al could join up and do right well," Pete offered. "Al has always been the luckiest among us. You'd be better off anyway."

Charley's voice became rough. "Don't you give me that talk! You just keep a sharp eye out for trouble, and if it comes, fire some shots down into the canyon so's we know there's trouble up here. Then run. Promise me you'll run."

"I promise," Pete said after a long pause.

Charley looked much relieved. "Good. Wish us luck down there."

"I wish you luck."

Charley nodded, and then he turned his back on his partner and headed for his burro. He had studied the trail they intended to follow down into the Grand Canyon, and he'd never seen anything in his whole life that looked scarier. But there was no turning back now. Besides, if a woman as soft and pretty as Lucy Holland had the stomach to take that trail, he guessed he did, too.

Since Al Holland was the only one of them who'd already made the giddy descent to the bottom of the Grand Canyon, he volunteered to take the lead, and no one objected. Behind Al went Lucy and then Charley, Zeke, and finally the Gunsmith, all of them leading burros.

"Don't look down," Al shouted back to them. "Just keep your eyes on the trail."

"What about the burros?" Charley asked.

"If one gives us trouble, we'll blindfold him, and if that don't work, push him over. But no matter what, don't let the sonofabitches pull you over the side or slam into the animal behind and knock it off the edge."

Everyone nodded, because Al's advice made plenty of sense. Lucy looked pale and Clint was cotton-mouthed as they started down. He tried not to look over the edge of the trail, but there was something about the terrible height that drew his eyes like steel to a magnet. And each time he did glance over the side, he regretted it. Once, at a place where the trail was no more than two feet wide due to a washout, the men in front almost lost their nerve. Clint saw Al hesitate, then force himself and his brave little burro onward.

The burros were magnificent. With their little heads bobbing up and down, they stepped as carefully as if they were walking through a bed of scattered coals. Not once did Clint's burro crowd or in any other way cause him to lose his own concentration. This was a trail that not even the most experienced trail horse could have navigated, but the little burros descended the steep, winding path that dropped hundreds of feet into the earth as if they did it every day of their lives.

It was midafternoon before they finally reached the bottom. The air was considerably warmer than it had been up on the rim, and with their coats on, they were all sweating profusely, as much from the warmer air as from the ordeal they'd just completed.

"I don't even want to think about having to climb back out of here," Clint said, shielding his eyes and gazing up the steep cliffsides.

"Then don't," Al advised. "We got more than our share of problems down here already without worrying about how we're going to get out."

Al led them on down to the river. It was red and roiling, powerful and loud. Clint saw driftwood hanging high and dry up on the canyon walls and commented on it to Al.

"This time of year," the prospector said, "the river is way low. Now, in the spring, the water will rise along this section of canyon so that we'd be ten, maybe even fifteen feet under water right now."

"What about the Indians that live in this canyon?" Lucy asked, gazing around at the red rock walls that seemed in danger of collapsing in on them.

"There are places where they live up high. This canyon has hundreds of smaller canyons leading into it. The Indians live up those canyons, and there's plenty of wild game and the fishing is always good. It's just that, at certain low times of the year like right now, parts of this canyon are underwater."

Clint nodded. "So what now?"

"We find Shorty's body," Al said. "And then I bury what's left of him."

"Yeah," Clint said, embarrassed because he'd forgotten about the poor old prospector who'd been riddled by arrows and whose body had been hanging for weeks over the canyon floor.

Grim-faced, Al led them along narrow trails back upriver. Clint was looking for signs of Indians, and the old man was scanning the canyon walls, searching for the landmarks to show him the place where his dead companion had fallen.

"There!" Al said, pointing up the canyon side. "See the trail we was on?"

Clint had to strain his eyes to see the trail where he and Al had almost lost their lives attempting to hoist up Shorty's body. It was no more than a thin pencil line on a rock wall.

"Yeah," he said at last.

"The body will be over there in that brush," Al said.

Clint hesitated. "I better go and help him," he said, handing the lead rope of his burro to Lucy.

"Give him a few minutes to be alone with Shorty," Lucy said.

Clint guessed that she was right. So he stood beside

Lucy and lost himself in the huge canyon, watching how the colors of shifting sunlight were constantly changing the hues of the rocks. The more he watched, the more he appreciated how truly spectacular the Grand Canyon was and why it deserved to be considered one of nature's greatest wonders.

"I guess he's probably ready for your help," Lucy said quietly.

Clint had brought an extra blanket, and now he untied it and carried it up to the body. Al had covered his dead partner with his own coat, and the old man's face was deeply etched with grief. Clint used the blanket to wrap what was left of Shorty.

"He saved my life," Al said brokenly. "He was the best friend I've ever had."

Clint didn't know what to say, so he remained silent. He just wrapped the body up and helped Al carry it down to a sandy place along the river. Next he got a pick and shovel, and they buried the old prospector quickly.

"You go on ahead until sundown and find a camp," Al choked. "I'll be along."

Lucy touched her father's arm. "Maybe I should stay with you."

"No," Al said, "I'll be all right. You go on now. Find a good camp where we can build a fire under the rocks that won't light up the canyon's walls."

Lucy left her father beside the fresh grave and followed Clint, Charley, and Zeke on up the canyon. None of them were feeling in good spirits. They were all thinking of Shorty's body that had been shot full of arrows and then smashed on the rocks. Clint just hoped the old man really had saved the last bullet for himself—just as he would do if it came right down to the end and there was no chance of survival, only torture and a slow, cruel death.

FOURTEEN

They slept late the next morning, lulled by the steady drone of the mighty Colorado and fooled by the late-morning shadows of the towering cliffs surrounding them.

After eating a quick breakfast, they moved out, heading steadily upriver and ever alert for signs of Indians.

"In this deep canyon," Al explained, "there are so many bends and rocks that you can pass your enemy by a hundred yards and never see or hear him."

"Then that's a factor in our favor," Clint said, his Winchester never far from reach.

They had their work cut out for them. The canyon floor, littered with driftwood from previous floods, was a tangle that defied all but the most strenuous efforts. The little burros that had so adeptly picked their way down the steep canyon side now found themselves struggling to leap over piles of wood and sometimes were even forced to swim through cold, clear pools or rushing streams that fed the Grand Canyon from a thousand mysterious canyons.

"A man," Clint observed, "could easily spend his life exploring these side canyons, some of them big enough to hide entire armies."

"And Indian villages," Zeke said cryptically. "Al, any

idea where those Indians that almost killed you are settled?"

"Up ahead," the prospector replied.

"Then why are we going that way!"

"Because," Al said, "that's got to be close to where the
Spanish fortune is hidden."

Clint studied Lucy's pretty face. She had lost some
weight since leaving her saloon and dancehall behind.
They had been on the trail for nearly a week, and she'd
proven herself a real trooper, though. Lucy hadn't complained and she hadn't slowed them down, even a bit. In
fact, Clint admired the way she seemed to actually thrive
on the hardships they faced daily.

"I grew up with it," Lucy explained later that morning.
"My father has always been a prospector. My mother died
when I was very young, and so I had no choice but to follow Father around the wilderness, searching for gold."

"A hard life for a little girl."

"No," she said, smiling at Clint, "it was a wonderful
life. I always had my own pet burro. I could ride him when
I grew tired of walking. I trapped desert rats and mice,
played with tortoises, and learned to avoid rattlesnakes
and scorpions. The high desert we usually roamed always
had wild mustangs to chase and admire. I think I had the
most wonderful childhood imaginable. Not many friends
my own age, but the old prospectors, most of whom are
now dead, pampered me shamelessly. I was their pet."

Clint was filled with admiration for this woman.
"You're nobody's pet now," he said, his eyes sliding
over the tight-fitting men's jeans she wore. "And I think
you're also a hell of a lot of woman."

Lucy squeezed his hand. "It's been a rough journey so
far. But maybe if we have some time to sneak away this
evening, we could go for a swim together."

Clint grinned. "The air is warm down here, but the water is pretty damn cold."

"Then we'd just have to warm each other up when we got out, wouldn't we," she breathed.

Clint gulped and felt himself fill out his trousers a little. "Yeah," he said, "I guess we would at that."

It was late afternoon when Al, in the lead, suddenly threw up his hand in warning and then pulled his burro back behind a rock and out of sight.

Zeke started to curse, but Al clamped a hand over his mouth. Clint dragged his burro up beside the others, then inched around the rocks with the rifle in his fist.

Indians! There were about fifteen of them, about half a mile upriver, spearing fish in a shallow side pool. Clint watched them carefully and was soon joined by Al and Lucy.

"Zeke is handling the burros," Lucy whispered in Clint's ear.

Clint nodded in understanding. His eyes searched the area, looking for the Indians' camp, but he didn't see any smoke or other sign of habitation.

"Al, you got any idea where they're camped?" he asked.

Al pointed up a deep canyon. "There's a village about a mile up that canyon. A big one."

"Are these the same bunch that came after you and Shorty?"

"Yeah." Al clenched the rifle in his fist so hard that his knuckles went white. "And I sure would like to open fire and take as many as I could right now."

"You'd be sentencing us to death," Clint said bluntly. "Where do you think the Spanish treasure is hidden?"

"Farther upriver. A couple of miles ahead there's a place where another big river joins the Colorado, and right where they meet, there's an old Spanish coat of arms with a tree growing up through it."

"I heard about that," Clint said. "So where do you think the treasure is exactly?"

"I ain't sure," Al admitted. "But I swear to you that I could smell it. Shorty and I were *that close*."

Clint shook his head. "The trouble is, these Indians are also real damned close."

"So what are we going to do?" Zeke asked.

Everyone looked to Clint for the answer, and he squirmed a little under their glare. What he wanted to say was that no treasure on earth was worth the risk of continuing on up this awesome canyon. Instead, he cleared his throat and said, "We'll just have to wait until after dark and then sneak by."

"But they'll see our tracks tomorrow morning," Charley protested.

"Not if we stay in the river."

They all studied the river. In some places it was just too swift to enter, but in others, it was quite placid. Unfortunately, the stretch for the next mile ahead looked swift and difficult.

"We don't have any choice but to try or turn back," Clint said. "Which is it to be?"

"We'll try it," Charley said.

"Yeah," Al said. "We come too far to turn back now."

Clint sighed in resignation. "Lucy?"

"We have to try," she said. "If we can get around that next bend in the river, we'll be out of danger."

"Unless there's another village up ahead we don't know about," Clint groused.

"You sure are one to look at the dark side of things, aren't you," Al snapped.

"You bet I am," Clint said. "I expect the worst, and

that's the only reason I'm still alive. Only fools expect difficult things to turn out easy. That water we'll have to enter is swift, and it will take everything we have just to keep ourselves and the burros from losing their footing and getting swept downriver."

"We could rope ourselves together," Lucy suggested.

Clint nodded his approval of the idea. He'd cut the rope from Shorty's battered body before they'd buried the prospector, and they'd brought a few extra ropes for climbing or solving problems exactly like this.

Clint glanced up at the sky, then back at the Indians. They were slender, supple brown men. Short of stature with slightly bowed legs, their torsos were thick and their arms were sinewy. Clint judged that they would not weigh an average of much over a hundred pounds, but from the way they used their spears and nimbly hopped from rock to rock, it was clear that they were well adapted to this starkly beautiful canyon and they would be formidable opponents.

"We might as well relax," Lucy said. "It'll be several hours before darkness sets in."

"I'm going to take a nap," Zeke announced, and he slid back from the rocks.

"Guess I will too," Al said. "Especially since we won't be getting much sleep tonight."

"What about you, Lucy?"

She looked at Clint. "There was another nice pool of water we passed just up above those rocks. I was thinking about taking a bath."

Al Holland raised his eyebrows. "A bath?"

"Sure."

"What for! You'll just get dirty again tomorrow."

"Maybe so," Lucy told her father, "but I'll feel better until I do."

Al shook his head in amazement, and then he went hobbling over to join Charley and Zeke and take a nap.

"What about you, Clint?" Lucy asked. "You like to take a little bath with me?"

"Damn fine idea," he said. "If we're going to drown tonight or get scalped tomorrow, I'd like to think I had a little pleasure before cashing in my chips and that this whole fiasco wasn't a total waste of time."

Lucy took his hand. "Well," she said, "I think I can handle that."

Fifteen minutes later, they had hiked upriver and rounded a bend where the whole world seemed to be theirs alone. They stripped off their clothes and dove into a side pool, laughing and frolicking together and working very hard not to think about the dangers they would face in the next twenty-four hours.

"Come here," Clint said, and Lucy swam over to him.

"You want something?" she asked coyly.

"Damn right I do."

Clint did not mess around with any foreplay. He eased Lucy into shallow water and mounted her with great urgency. She was no less enthusiastic, as her lovely legs wrapped around his waist and her pelvis began to thrust against his with great force.

"Just look at it!" she said throatily, as he worked over her with deep thrusts. "It's like we are making love in a cathedral. Isn't that a terribly sacrilegious thought?"

He slowed the rotation of his hips and twisted his head around. "I think this is the most natural place to make love in the whole wide world."

"Really?"

"Yes," he grunted, his mouth finding and ravishing her large breasts.

Lucy closed her eyes and moaned with pleasure. "We're muddying the river," she whispered.

"It's a big river and it's already muddy," he said, enjoying himself more and more, his entire body starting to tingle with exquisite pleasure.

Lucy suddenly bucked and rolled in the water, and Clint let out a yelp as he found himself on his back. "Hey, what's the idea!"

"Can you feel it?" she asked sweetly.

"What, your body pulling me deep inside?"

"That too, but I was thinking of the nice way the sand scratches your back. Doesn't that feel wonderful?"

Clint growled from way down in his throat. He reached up and filled his hands with Lucy's sweet buttocks and pulled them tightly down on his thrusting manhood.

"Honey," he groaned, "the only thing I can feel right now is *you*."

Lucy kissed him passionately, and a moment later they were making big waves on the muddy Colorado.

FIFTEEN

Clint glanced up at the stars. The Indians who had been spearfishing had disappeared at sundown, and for the last three hours, the only sound or movement in the canyon was that of the mighty Colorado River. In the moon- and starlight, the Gunsmith could see the roiling white water of the rapids that they were about to enter.

"I'll go in first, leading my burro," he said. "I'll do my damnedest to stay right next to the shore, where the water isn't so swift. If I make it around, I'll leave the burro and come back down to help the rest of you."

Zeke, Al, Charley, and Lucy, each nodded. It was clear that they doubted the Gunsmith could wade the Colorado without being caught in its swift current and sent spinning downriver.

"Clint?"

He turned to Lucy, and she took his hands in her own. "Clint, maybe you were right. Maybe we should just turn around and forget all this treasure business."

"What's the matter?" he asked. "Are you getting cold feet?"

"I don't want you to drown in that torrent."

"I'm a pretty fair swimmer. If I lose my footing, I'll

117

at least have a fighting chance."

"But—"

Clint cut off Lucy's protest. "If it's impossible out there, I'll turn my burro around and come back. Maybe we can hike along the riverbank and attempt to hide our tracks."

"You said that would be impossible."

Clint smiled grimly. "Yeah, I did, didn't I?"

She kissed his lips and released him. Clint took his burro and led it down to the river's edge. He wasn't at all confident he could make it upriver. At a dozen places he could see that big boulders and rocks jutted far out into the current. They had to be circumvented, and that would take him much deeper into the river than he cared to venture.

The burro balked, and it took all of them to push the protesting little animal into the water. Once in the river, the animal began to hop and flounder, and it took all of Clint's effort to keep his own balance while also trying to control the terrified little beast.

The water was swift and cold. He finally got the burro moving behind him as he waded upriver. The first hundred yards went just fine. Even the little burro seemed to gain confidence. Clint kept within a few yards of the riverbank where the river was no more than three feet deep, except when he stepped into an occasional hole and found himself gasping and swimming, his boots scrambling for a foothold.

"Damn!" he swore, each time he dropped in over his head and had to thrash his way back to solid footing. "I must be out of my mind to be doing this!"

Still, he was making progress, until he came to the first big boulder that he would have to skirt. He could see the river pounding the boulder, sending water splashing upward.

"We got no choice but to try and get around it," he

said, edging out farther into the current, until it was up to his waist and pulling strongly against him.

The burro would not go any farther. When the water reached its belly, it buried its hooves into the shifting bed of the river and refused to go another step.

"Come on!" Clint shouted over the roar of water as he pulled with all his strength. But the burro would not move.

Dripping wet and exasperated, Clint reckoned he had just two choices: Turn around, or say to hell with it and wade ashore wherever the river was too dangerous. Clint chose the latter alternative.

"Let's go," he said, pulling the burro back on shore and circumventing the boulder to continue on up the river.

Once the decision was made to use the shore whenever the water became too deep or swift, Clint felt much better. He and his burro went about a mile and a half upriver until he was safely past the side canyon leading up to the Indian village before he tied the burro under some cover.

"I'll be back soon," he promised, shivering from the cold but determined to go back and get the rest of his party safely past danger.

When Clint returned, Lucy threw herself into his arms. "We thought surely you must have drowned!"

"I would have," he admitted, "if I'd tried to stay in the river. But my burro was smarter than I was and refused, so I took to the shore."

Al shook his head. "So we'll leave tracks. You know we can't brush or hide them all. Sooner or later—and I'm pretty damned sure it will be sooner—one of those sharp-eyed Indians will see something that will sound the alert. They'll come after us."

"What other choice do we have?" Clint asked. "It's impossible to stay in the water and get around some of those big boulders. The river is too swift and deep."

"I could have told you that before you took off," Charley said.

Clint frowned. "Why don't we get going. Once we're all a good distance above the Indians' side canyon, then I'll have to come back and do my best to wipe out our tracks. We sure as hell won't get much sleep tonight."

"We're not here to sleep," Zeke grumped.

Clint said nothing. Al and Zeke were old and tired and getting grumpy. They were wound up tight as a watch spring, and every mile they went took them farther into the canyon and farther away from where Pete waited on top with the horses. There seemed to be a growing danger in every turn of this great canyon. And yet, none of them were of a mind to turn around and return to Apache Junction.

"Let's go," Clint said, taking Lucy's burro and tying one end of a rope to her waist and the other to his own. "Just stay real close. If you lose your footing and go down, grab something and I'll pull you up to me."

"All right," she promised.

Clint led the second burro into the river, and it also balked, though not as strenuously as the first. And once the second animal was in the water, Zeke, Charley, and Al had no difficulty getting their burros to follow.

"Stay right behind me," Clint yelled. "There are some underwater potholes that I discovered the hard way. Just stay in single file and we'll do fine."

This time, Clint found the going a little easier. He was freezing cold and his teeth were chattering, but he knew the holes, and when he came to the first big boulder, he did not hesitate to angle in to the shore. He was just coming out of the river when he heard Zeke shout for help.

Clint twisted around to see that the old prospector had

ventured too far out into the current. He and his burro
were being pulled out into the river.

"Help!" Zeke cried.

Clint grabbed the rope that linked him to Lucy and tried
to untie the knot. But his fingers were numb with cold, and
so he stood helplessly as Zeke and the burro were whisked
out into the current.

Al Holland shouted and then dropped his lead rope. He
lunged out into the river in an insane attempt to rescue
Zeke.

Clint went after Lucy's father. He hit the end of his rope
just as his fingers buried themselves into Al's jacket.

"Are you crazy!" he screamed at the old prospector.

Al struggled mightily, and Clint could feel Lucy pulling
both he and her father ever so slowly toward shore.

"Help!" Zeke cried again as he and his thrashing burro
vanished around a bend in the river and disappeared.

Al was thrashing and yelling at the top of his lungs, but
Clint refused to let the old man go free. When Al tried
to knock him loose, Clint yanked his Colt from his soggy
holster and pistol-whipped the old man across the back of
the head. Al went limp, and before his head sank below
the surface of the river, Clint grabbed him and dragged
him back to shore.

"Did you have to use your pistol on him?" Lucy
screamed.

Clint stood shaking and gazing downriver. The moon-
and starlight bathed the surface in a soft patina of silver.
Zeke was gone. Neither he nor his burro would have lasted
two hundred yards in those terrible rapids.

"Well, did you!" Lucy cried.

Clint turned back to see Lucy glaring at him. "Yes, I
did," Clint said, trying to keep his teeth from rattling.
"Now, let's get him lashed down on his burro and let's

get out of here! We've still got to try and hide our tracks before daylight or we're all dead."

Lucy shook herself as if she might emerge from a bad dream. Then she and Charley helped Clint get her father slung across the top of his burro. They used their rope to tie Al down before they resumed their slow, difficult journey upriver.

When Clint had everyone safely upriver from the Indian village, he retraced his path. There were a good half-dozen places where they'd been forced out of the river and onto shore. Clint started working on the one farthest downriver and nearest to the side pool where they'd watched the Indians spearfishing.

He cut himself a thick branch of sagebrush and used it to scrape and brush all their tracks away as best he could. If he'd have thought to bring canteens, he would also have poured water over the tracks to wipe them out, but since he had not, he hoped that the sagebrush would leave no signs. The deepest tracks were made by the hoofprints of the burros. Each one of these actually had to be filled in with mud and then brushed over.

Fortunately, the moonlight was good enough to work by, and it took Clint the remainder of the night to cover their tracks. When he had finally worked his way back upriver to the others, they were huddled, shivering and angry under some rocks.

"We'd better push on," Clint said. "The more distance we can put between ourselves and that Indian village, the better off we will be."

Lucy said nothing. She climbed to her feet and helped Al to his. Both looked broken in spirit, totally demoralized by what had happened to Zeke.

"Listen," Clint said roughly, "I told you that some of us were not going to climb out of this canyon. Spanish gold or no Spanish gold, we have gone too far now to turn back or even second-guess ourselves. To be blunt, we've paid our ante and we're up to our necks in this card game. It's just win or lose now. Nothing in between. We either live—or we die."

Lucy raised her head and stared at him. "So," she said, her voice shaking with anger, "you predicted that we would come to regret this, and you were right. Now you seem to almost gloat over the situation."

Clint shook his head. If he'd had the time or the strength, he'd have thrown Lucy over his knee and given her a sound paddling.

"I'm not gloating about anything!" he said in anger. "But I'll tell you this: Either we start thinking less of Spanish gold and more of how to get out of this canyon, or we're as good as dead."

Lucy, Charley, and Al said nothing. They didn't have to. Clint could see by the shocked looks on their numb faces that they knew he was telling them the truth.

SIXTEEN

By his third day on the rim, Pete was growing increasingly worried about what might have happened to his friends down in the canyon. He knew that they had gone west to the better trail leading down to the canyon floor. Once they reached it, they'd come back upriver and pass underneath Pete; and now they were probably somewhere to the east of him.

Pete was torn with indecision. Now that he'd rested, he'd grown increasingly apprehensive. Where were his friends now? Had they discovered the Spanish treasure or had—God forbid—they been attacked by Indians and perhaps slaughtered down in one of the deep, shadowy canyons that fed into the Grand Canyon?

Waiting was the hardest thing that Pete had ever done. Like most prospectors, he was a fidgety man, always pulling up stakes from one disappointing claim to search for another.

So it was that, by late afternoon on the third day of his vigil, Pete decided he could not possibly wait another minute.

"Duke," he said, catching up Clint's fine gelding, "you and me and Miss Lucy's fine little mare are going to go searchin'. I figure they're upriver somewhere, and the closer that I keep to them, the better off we'll all be."

Duke was unaccustomed to the strange rider, but since Pete was now very familiar and had even spent time talking to him during the last three days, the gelding did not fight the man. Instead, Duke behaved when the old prospector struggled his way up into the saddle.

"You're sure a tall feller," Pete said, gathering his reins and then dallying the mare's lead rope to his saddlehorn and reining east to follow the Colorado upriver.

All that day he kept stopping to peer over the canyon's lip in the desperate hope of seeing Clint, Lucy, Al, Charley, or Zeke. But he had no luck, and that night when he camped, he was discouraged and losing hope that his friends were still alive.

Pete slept poorly and awoke before dawn. At first light he shot a rabbit and made a fire, then cleaned the rabbit and set about to roast it over the coals.

Two miles behind him, Wallace Boggs was roused out of his sleep by one of his hired guns.

"Mr. Boggs, I heard a rifleshot to the east of us! And look, do you see that thin trail of smoke!"

Boggs shielded his eyes because he was staring directly into the sunrise. And as the other hired gunmen around him began to chatter with excitement, Boggs squinted hard; still he did not see the trail of smoke, but the gunmen did.

"All right," he said, trying to clear his head. "It's *got* to be them."

"But why'd they be on the rim still?" one of his men asked.

It was a good and obvious question, and Boggs was angry he hadn't thought of it himself. "Well . . . well how the hell should I know? But maybe they've already been down in the Grand Canyon, gotten out the Spanish gold, and are about to leave."

"That don't seem too likely," another man said. "Unless they got real lucky."

"If they did, then we're the ones who are going to be in luck," Boggs said.

"What about Timberman?"

Boggs frowned. He needed Timberman's gun and that of the six men who rode with him. "Luke," he said, "you go back and find Ulysses and tell him to come running."

Luke made it clear that he did not like the idea of turning back and perhaps missing the chance to be the first to get his hands on the Spanish gold.

"I'd rather go ahead with you, Mr. Boggs. Timberman will figure out that he's going off in the wrong direction soon enough. And you might need all of our guns."

Boggs had to agree that the man was probably right. "Okay," he said, climbing stiffly out of his bedroll and choking back a groan. He had saddle sores on saddle sores. He was stove up from sleeping on the hard ground and just plenty pissed off about everything in general.

"Saddle up my horse," he muttered to no one in particular. "We'll leave just as soon as I've had some coffee."

The hired gunmen looked disgusted, but since Boggs was paying their wages, no one dared to object. Instead they saddled Boggs's horse and settled down to wait impatiently as he downed three cups of steaming black coffee.

"All right," he muttered almost thirty minutes later, "let's ride."

They rode out with Boggs in the lead. The insides of his legs were chaffed so badly they seemed to be on fire and his butt felt like sausage. Still, he took heart in the fact that he might just be about to overtake the Gunsmith, Lucy, and those four old men. But even more important, maybe they had already found the Spanish gold and it would be theirs for the taking.

Pete sensed rather than heard the approaching riders. One minute he was wrapping his lips around the steaming carcass of his roast rabbit, the next minute he was dropping the greasy critter into the fire and snatching up his rifle.

Boggs and his men were about a mile distant and coming fast. Pete only had enough time to bridle Duke, then tear hobbles from the gelding and Lucy's mare.

Before mounting, Pete threw his Winchester to his shoulder and took aim at the thick body of Wallace Boggs. When he fired, he had the great satisfaction of seeing Apache Junction's mayor grab his shoulder and then topple from his horse. Two more bullets scattered the attacking force, and, fed by adrenaline, Pete somehow mounted the tall black gelding and raced away, leading the mare.

"Whoo-weee!" he shouted, looking back over his shoulder to see that three of Boggs's hired gunmen were still on his tail but that the others had gathered around their wounded leader.

Pete had to keep Duke from running away from the mare. He kept checking the powerful gelding, aware that he needed to pace his flight or he'd run both of his horses into the earth.

The men chasing him were falling behind, and after two miles, it occurred to Pete that he was leading them in the direction of his friends, still lost in the canyon below.

Pete reined Duke to a standstill. His skinny legs gripped the barrel of the sweating horse as he quickly weighed his next move. If he kept racing east along the canyon's rim, he might expose his friends below. But if he turned south toward Apache Junction, they'd know he was trying to lead them away from the Gunsmith and the treasure.

"So what the hell should I do!" he cried in frustration. There was no choice but to keep going east. At some point he would no doubt see the Gunsmith and his party far below, and then he could decide what to do next. One thing for sure: He had actually put a bullet into Wallace Boggs and maybe even killed him. That alone made whatever else might happen to him worth the game.

A bullet whistled past his head. Pete put his reins between his teeth and tried to take aim with his rifle. He fired two quick shots; neither of them came near to hitting his targets, but they did manage to bring the attackers up short.

"Come and get me, you bloodthirsty bastards!" Pete shouted.

Boggs's men answered in lead, and because they were hired guns, their bullets were too close for comfort, so Pete reined Duke about and continued on to the east. The marksmen wheeled their horses around and went back to see their fallen leader.

"I hope he dies slow," Pete said hoarsely, as he continued deeper into the wild country that lay ahead. "No matter what happens to me, killin' the almighty Mayor Boggs would make it all worthwhile."

About sundown, Pete topped a low rise and there before him stretched another big, bright red river leading down into the Grand Canyon.

"My Lord!" Pete exclaimed, noting how the river flowed between two humped red hills. "That's it!"

In the fading light of day, his old eyes searched for the tree that grew up through a coat of rusting Spanish armor. But he couldn't spot it.

No matter. This *was* the place. Pete could feel it in his brittle old bones. The place that was very near the lost Spanish treasure of the Grand Canyon.

SEVENTEEN

When Clint hurled the branch of sagebrush that he'd been using into the Colorado River, it was almost daybreak. He was dog-tired from lack of sleep and from the ordeal of getting Lucy, her father, Charley and their burros past the Indians. As for covering their tracks, he wasn't sure if his efforts had been successful or not. The moonlight had been bright enough to see the tracks, but if the sharp-eyed canyon Indians noticed the brushmarks on the sandy shore, they'd know that something was very much amiss and come searching for intruders.

"We've got to keep moving," Clint said.

"What about Zeke?" Lucy blurted.

"What about him?"

Lucy raised her hands and dropped them at her sides in a gesture of futility. "It just seems like we ought to do *something*."

Clint expelled a deep breath. "Zeke is gone. No man could have survived those rapids. I just hope he died quickly and that the Indians don't find his body or that of his burro hung up on some rocks."

"And if they do they'll know that we're upriver of their camp."

"That's right," Clint said. "The way I figure it, either the burro or old Zeke will probably wash up on a log or some rocks and their bodies will be found. What it means is that we are down to just the four of us."

"Five," Lucy said, "counting Pete."

"Pete is up there," Clint said, pointing westward along the rim. "And I hope for his sake and ours that he stays up there and doesn't try to come down. At any rate, he can't help us. He'll be lucky if he can stay out of Ulysses Timberman's way."

Lucy's fists clenched at her sides. "You were right and we were wrong about coming here! This canyon and the damned Spanish gold has already claimed the lives of Shorty and now Zeke. No amount of gold is worth it."

Up to this time, Clint had felt admiration and, of course, a strong physical attraction for Lucy, but now he was feeling compassion as well. "We all make mistakes. There was no way of knowing we'd lose Zeke."

"Yes there was," Lucy said. "You warned us before we left that some of us would not return to Apache Junction. And you were right. The thing that I'm afraid of is that *none* of us will make it out of this damned canyon."

Clint could see that Lucy was close to the breaking point. He took her hands in his own. "We'll make it," he promised. "I'm not saying we'll find that Spanish gold, but we'll make it out with our lives."

She forced a smile. "We'd better get moving. You're right about those Indians probably finding a body in the river."

Clint nodded and walked over to Al Holland. "How much farther do we have to go before we come to that Spanish suit of armor near which you think the gold is hidden?"

"Down here in this canyon, I can't see any landmarks,"

Al said quietly, his own spirits low because of Zeke's death. "But I'd say that it can't be more than a few more miles up this river."

"Let's hope not," Clint said, as he took his burro's lead rope and turned upriver.

All afternoon the going was tough, as they circled boulders and fought their way through driftwood and massive, shattered, and tangled logs that might well have originated in the Rocky Mountains and been swept down the Colorado during times of flood. Sometimes they found that they had little choice but to wade out into the cold river, and whenever that happened, the poor burros protested, and by late afternoon, Clint guessed that they'd probably made a grand total of five miles' progress up the river.

"Clint?"

He turned to see Lucy gazing at her father, who was staring at the south rim. Clint frowned. He was wet, cold, and exhausted, and it was quite likely that there were Indians coming after them from down here in the canyon and white men flanking them from up above.

"What's wrong?"

Al raised his finger. "Look. Do you see them?"

With the canyon walls towering over them, Clint had no idea what the man was referring to. "Do I see what?"

"Those two red hills!"

"Yeah. Just the tops of them."

"They're the ones. Between them flows a red river, and where it joins with the Colorado is where we'll find the suit of Spanish armor. The treasure can't be more than a few hundred yards from there."

"How can you be sure?"

The old man tore his eyes off the red hills. "I can't explain my reasoning. It's just a gift that I have. Shorty had it; so did Zeke and even Pete. You just sort of develop

a sixth sense about gold after you've been searching for it
long enough."

Clint thought that was hogwash. If it were true, then
why were all the old prospectors he'd ever seen still pen-
niless? But the good news was that if they were almost
to the place where Al was sure he could find the Spanish
treasure, then they could finally settle this issue once and
for all.

"If we don't run into too many more obstacles and we
aren't overtaken by the Indians, maybe we can be there
an hour or so before dark."

"Yeah," Al said, a strange light coming into his eyes.
"And with any luck, I might even find the treasure before
nightfall."

Clint did not share that hope, but since nothing was to
be gained by expressing his doubts, he simply nodded and
continued slowly picking a way for them upriver.

Just before dusk, the canyon opened a little and they
rounded a bend in the river, and there flowed another river
into the Colorado, one even redder.

"Look!" cried Lucy. "It's Pete and the horses!"

Clint's face split into a wide grin. He was as happy
to see Duke as he was the old prospector. Suddenly, it
appeared as if perhaps they really would live to tell about
this great Grand Canyon treasure hunt. All four of them
ran to greet the prospector, but as they drew closer, Pete's
grin died.

"Where's Zeke!" the old man shouted, his words echoing up and down the canyon walls.

"He's gone," Al said. "Washed downriver."

Pete blinked as if he'd been bludgeoned. "Zeke is dead?"

"Yeah," Charley said. "Him and his burro both went
into the water. There was nothing we could do to save
them. There was rapids and . . . "

Pete turned away to hide his tears. Clint watched the old man's body quiver, and he heard Pete sniffle. Soon, however, the prospector gathered his composure.

"They're right behind me," he said. "I shot the mayor. Don't know if he's dead. But the rest will be coming along."

Clint swore in silence. There was no useful purpose to be served by berating Pete about leading Timberman and the others right to this place. Pete was already devastated by the loss of his friend.

"What are we going to do?" Lucy asked.

"The only thing we can do is to get out of this canyon fast and hope we can somehow strike out across country and manage to throw them off our backtrail."

"Oh, no!" Al swore. "I lost my partner and now Pete has lost his friend, and we'll be damned if we're going to give up on the treasure now that we're finally here!"

"Then you'll be damned if you do and dead if you don't," Clint said hotly. "You're not going to be satisfied until we're all dead—including your daughter!"

"Stop it!" Lucy cried.

Clint was furious. "This whole deal is snake-bitten. It started out bad and it's getting worse. If the Indians catch us down here tomorrow morning we're finished, and if they don't, you can bet Timberman and his men will."

Al Holland stood his ground. "I'm staying until I find that lost treasure."

"So am I," Pete said.

Clint walked over to his horse. He didn't bother to ask what had happened to his fine saddle. It was gone, just like the chance of surviving this mess.

"Lucy, your horse is sound, and if we get out of this canyon tonight, we've got a good chance of staying alive. But if we wait . . . "

"I *can't* leave them!"

"Damnation!" Clint swore. "Al, talk to your daughter. Make her see the truth of it. You and Pete are old men. You've almost lived your lives to their full span. But your daughter is young. She deserves to live to be old. Make her come away with me."

Al turned to his daughter, and his voice sounded almost tragic. "Lucy," he said, "the Gunsmith is right. If you remain here, you'll likely be killed tomorrow. So go with him."

"No!"

Al's voice hardened. "I'm telling you to ride away with him right now!"

"I won't do it!" Lucy shook her head. "I'm not a child any more, to be ordered around. I can make up my own mind, and I'm staying until we all go at once."

"The hell with it," Clint said, dropping the rope to the burro and hopping on Duke's back. "You're all gold-fevered fools. I'm getting out of here while I still can."

Clint hesitated. His eyes locked with those of Lucy, and he wanted to try one more time to make her see how senseless it was for her to throw her life away for the chance of gold. But Lucy wouldn't look directly at him, so he reined Duke away and rode up the red river toward a place where it was clear that he could escape the Grand Canyon.

Two hours later he was on the high rim of the canyon, and about a mile away, he saw the flickering campfire of his enemies, Boggs and Timberman. Good sense told Clint to ride quietly past and on into the desert. He was as good as free. But if he rode off and left Lucy, Al, Charley and Pete to the mercy of Boggs, that evil marshal, and the rest of his crowd, Clint knew that he'd never be able to look himself in the mirror. He'd always remember how pretty

Lucy had been and how she had loved him and made love to him. He'd wonder if Boggs and Timberman had killed her slow, or used her for their pleasure before killing her or even throwing her to the other men.

Clint shuddered. He simply could not ride away and have any respect for himself.

"Damnation!" he swore.

Clint reached down and checked his six-gun. It had been underwater a lot in the last few days, but he spun the cylinder and was certain that it would shoot just fine. He still had his rifle, too.

Well, Clint thought as he reined his horse toward the campfire of his enemies, let's just see how good a bunch of men we are up against.

EIGHTEEN

Clint tied Duke about a quarter of a mile from their camp and waited until he could see no moving shadows around the campfire, signaling that his enemies had gone to sleep. He removed his Stetson and, with his rifle gripped tightly in his hands, he crept forward in the moonlight, keeping low to the ground.

There were no guards, so Clint reached the perimeter of the campfire without incident. He counted seven sleeping bodies and immediately figured out that Marshal Timberman was not one of them, though the big form of Mayor Wallace Boggs was immediately identifiable. It was obvious to the Gunsmith that Timberman and Boggs had split their forces.

Clint's instincts told him that he could probably kill Boggs and at least three of the gunmen before they scattered and escaped. Maybe he could get them all if he was real lucky. The trouble was, Clint had never shot a sleeping man in his entire life, and the thought of starting now with half a dozen of them did not sit at all well. A few of the sleeping men were probably quite young and might even be salvageable human beings, given an opportunity.

Clint looked to their horses tied to a picket line with the thought of turning them loose. A man on foot in this country was in for a long, long walk. The trouble was, Ulysses Timberman and his force might be very close, and this bunch could simply double up on the gang's remaining horses.

Clint stretched out on the ground and concentrated on this knotty problem, even though his sleep-starved brain seemed incapable of rational thought. And the next thing he knew, the sun was rising in the east and someone was banging a pot of coffee over a fire.

In shock, Clint almost jumped to his feet, which would have been disastrous. Instead, he snatched up his Winchester and tried to slow his suddenly hammering heart, as he peered through the low brush and watched the camp prepare to ride.

It was clear that Boggs was in considerable pain, though not mortally wounded. He whined and was unwilling to do anything but order his sullen men around.

"I tell you," one of the men argued, "we need to send someone back after Marshal Timberman!"

"We shouldn't have let that old geezer on the black horse get away from us," another man swore.

"Yeah, well, how the hell were we supposed to catch him! Both his horses were fresher and faster than ours!"

Clint listened to the men argue for the next ten minutes, while he tried to figure out what it was he wanted to do. And then it came to him: He needed a cup of coffee and the chance to take Mayor Boggs as a hostage. Maybe if he did that, then the hired gunmen would realize that they would not get paid.

Clint frowned, unsure that his thinking was correct, but seeing no alternatives. His horse was too far away to reach without being spotted, and he'd already decided that slaughtering this bunch was not his style.

The hell with it! The aroma of fresh coffee was driving him wild. "Freeze!" he shouted, jumping to his feet with the rifle pressed to his shoulder.

Everyone turned like parts in the same machine, except for one man who was quicker thinking and who went for his sidearm. Clint's rifle belched smoke and flame. The quick-thinker grabbed his chest and crashed over backward, kicking in death and beating at the brush.

"Anyone else ready to join him in the Promised Land?" Clint asked.

Boggs, his face pale with pain, was the first to answer: "You'll hang for this! Hang!"

Clint merely scoffed at the threat. "I guess it's hard for you to imagine how little worried I am of a hangman's noose, given the circumstances."

He levered another shell into the chamber of the rifle and eased it into his left hand, then drew his six-gun. "Now, every one of you reach across his waist and pull your gun. No tricks, or you'll join your foolish friend."

Boggs and his gunmen could still hear the final death throes of their companion, and the choice they had seemed an easy one.

"What are you going to do with us?" Boggs demanded, after Clint had pushed them back and confiscated their weapons.

Clint moved cautiously over to the fire. "I guess I'll drink the rest of your coffee and think about it."

Boggs and his men watched sullenly as Clint poured, then slowly sipped their coffee. The Gunsmith made a real big show out of enjoying the coffee, and when he was finished, he poured another cup, and it steamed no less than the six men glaring at him across the campfire.

"Yes sir," Clint said, smacking his lips and grinning

like he'd been out all night chewing loco weed. "Out on the range, a good morning cup of coffee is worth more than whiskey. Don't you fellers agree?"

"You sonofabitch!" a man swore. "Put that rifle down and I'll brace you right now!"

Clint's smile remained frozen on his lips as he moved forward and then tossed his steaming cup of coffee in the man's face, causing him to scream and cover his eyes.

Clint walked back to the coffee pot and poured another cup. "Anyone else want to say something?"

No one did. Not even Boggs, whose shoulder was heavily bandaged. "You boys can sit down," Clint said after a few minutes. "I think we'll just spend the day resting."

"What!" Boggs roared. "You must be crazy!"

"Nope." Clint figured that the very best thing he could do right now was to give Lucy and her father an entire day to search for that Spanish treasure.

Come nightfall, he'd decide what to do with this bunch, and then he'd take an extra horse or two and ride back to join his friends in the Grand Canyon. At that point, they'd either load the Spanish gold on the burros and head back for Apache Junction or they'd ride away, even if Clint had to knock them out cold and tie them to their saddles.

Clint scooted over to a pack of grub and helped himself to a package of sourdough rolls and some beef.

"Yes sir," the Gunsmith said, with his mouth stuffed, "when you work for Mr. Boggs, you eat in style!"

If looks could have killed, the Gunsmith would have been six times dead. That tickled him plenty. Right at the moment, things were looking pretty damn good. He had salvaged a little sleep last night, drank all the strong black coffee he could stomach this morning, had plenty of good food, and now he held captive six plenty pissed-off scoundrels he could goad at his leisure. Other than making love to sweet Lucy, things simply did not get much better.

NINETEEN

By late afternoon, Clint was eager to get on the move. He'd marched everyone out to get Duke, then marched them back to camp. Wallace Boggs was in pain and his men were ready to explode. Again and again, they looked to the west, clearly hoping that any minute they would see Marshal Timberman and his riders appear.

"I guess," Clint said, finishing off another meal, "you boys are all expecting the Marshal to come riding out of the sunset, guns blazing to save your hides."

"You got that about right," Boggs spat. "And when he does get here, I hope he shoots you in the guts and you die slow."

"My oh my," Clint said with a shocked expression. "You sure are filled with venom, aren't you, Mayor Boggs. And I'll just bet that if you had that pair of fancy, pearl-handled six-guns, you'd even try and use them on me."

"I sure as hell would!"

Clint shook his head as if greatly saddened by this piece of harsh news. "Tell you what: Since you're all in such a big hurry to see Marshal Timberman again, start walking."

"What!"

Clint thumbed back the hammer of his pistol. "You heard me. Start walking!"

There was a sudden, deadly iron in Clint's voice that left no doubt in anyone's mind that he meant business.

Boggs's face flamed with outrage. "You're sending us off on foot and unarmed in this Indian country!"

"Yep. I figure you've got a better than even chance of stumbling on Marshal Timberman before the Indians find you. And besides, if the shoe was on the other foot, you'd have killed me and my friends. So it's time to stop the jawing and git!"

Boggs had little choice but to do as Clint ordered, and his men fell in behind him. Clint just hoped that Boggs and his men did not team up with Marshal Timberman before tomorrow so that he, Lucy, Charley, Pete, and old Al could put some miles between them and the Grand Canyon.

It was long after midnight when Clint dismounted back at the south rim. He stared down into the huge canyon and then back at the horses he'd strung together and brought along. Getting this string down into the canyon was going to be a neat trick, but he guessed it was one that he could accomplish. Actually, leaving the horses behind would have been a very bad mistake, because Boggs and his men would have recaptured them.

Using the light of the moon, Clint relocated the trail down to the red river that joined the Colorado. Had he not remembered so clearly the other trails he'd suffered leading directly into the Grand Canyon, this trail would have seemed treacherous and steep, but now he tackled it without reservation. Lucy's mare seemed to lure the other horses right along, and within an hour, they were all moving along the nameless red river that joined the Colorado just a few miles away.

At the junction of the two rivers, Clint picketed his string of horses and stood holding his reins, wondering which direction he should try first. It would have been easy to shout or draw his gun and fire a couple of shots into the air. That would have attracted plenty of attention. But something told him that it would also be very foolish and possibly even fatal if there were Indians in the vicinity. Clint's eye caught something strange and he walked closer, then shook his head in amazement.

"Why I'll be damned!" he whispered, staring at the rusted armor breastplate with the tree growing out of it. "The old man wasn't seeing things after all."

Clint began to search for tracks other than his own, and within twenty minutes he was moving toward a large side canyon. He was leading Duke when the big gelding suddenly stopped and its nostrils began to quiver with excitement.

"What is it?" Clint whispered. "Are they just up ahead of us?"

The gelding snorted, and Clint closed his hand over the animal's soft muzzle. After several moments, he mounted Duke and rode on up the side canyon, gun in hand, until Duke again stopped and threw his head. Clint knew that something was very wrong, so he dismounted and tied the horse in some thickets. Taking his time and watching his footing, he crept forward to see the dying fire of an Indian camp. Around the camp lay perhaps forty warriors.

Clint expelled a deep, quiet breath. He stared up the dark canyon and knew with growing dread that Lucy, Al, Charley and old Pete were trapped up there somewhere, without any way to escape. The Gunsmith also realized that there was no way that he could kill all these sleeping warriors. After several minutes of deliberation, he decided that the only alternative he had was to get past the Indians and bring his friends back down this canyon. If they could sneak past this camp before sunrise, they'd be able to reach their horses and have a good chance of escaping with their lives.

Getting past the Indians took time and almost more patience than Clint could muster. He moved slowly, each step taken with care, until at the end of almost an hour, he was finally above the encampment far enough that he figured he could make better time. When he came upon the burros, the litter animals looked at him and then closed their eyes and began to doze again.

Clint hurried past the burros, and the next thing he knew, Lucy was throwing herself into his arms and sobbing quietly on his shoulder.

"It's going to be all right," he promised, his eyes on the moon as he judged how much darkness yet remained. "We're getting out of here right now."

But Lucy shook her head. "They think they've found it," she told him. "My father, Charley, and Pete believe they've found the lost Spanish treasure!"

"I don't care if they've found a mountain of gold," Clint said. "There's an encampment of Indians not a mile from here and they're going to attack at daylight. We've got to get out of here right now!"

"Then talk to them!" Lucy said. "Make them understand the danger. All they can see is the fortune they've always been searching for and that is now right at their fingertips."

"Maybe I can make them understand the stakes are their lives," Clint said. "Take me to them now."

Lucy led him about two hundred yards up the canyon, around a pillar of worn rocks and across a little stream that trickled out of the mouth of a cave whose entrance was faintly illuminated. "They're in there digging right now," Lucy said.

"Lead the way."

The entrance to the cave was low enough that Clint had to stoop to enter. Inside, the air was dank and the Gunsmith could feel a cool breeze brush his face. He heard the distant sound of rocks being moved, and he hurried forward after Lucy.

The tunnel expanded rather than contracted. It widened into a large cavern, and at the far end, Clint saw Pete, Charley, and Al so busy attacking a pile of loose rock that they didn't notice Clint until he was right next to them.

"There's a band of Indians just down the canyon, and they'll attack at daylight. We're getting out of here right now."

The old men turned around. Even in the poor candle-light, Clint could see that something had altered their eyes and their faces. They still looked old, but somehow different. Al spoke first: "Behind this wall of loose shale is another tunnel, and in it is the lost Spanish treasure."

Clint shook his head. "Didn't you understand what I said? There's an encampment of Indians nearby! They'll attack at first light and they'll kill all of us if we don't escape now."

"You can hold them off, can't you?" Pete asked, licking his lips nervously. "If you could hold them off until—"

"I can't hold them off!" Clint stormed. "Are you crazy!"

In answer, the men turned their backs on him and returned to digging furiously at the pile of loose shale, tearing it away with their bare hands.

Clint knew he was wasting his breath. "You've gone crazy as loons over gold." He turned to Lucy. "I returned

because your life is very important to me. So is that of
your father, Charley and Pete. But I can't help them any
more. All I can do is get them out alive."

"And I can't leave them to die," she said quietly.

Clint shook his head as if he were locked into a nightmare. "Come over here so we can talk in private," he said,
leading the young woman back toward the entrance until
they were out of sight and hearing of the three madmen.

The moment they were alone, Clint said, "Give me a
hug good-bye."

Lucy ran into his outstretched arms, and as Clint hugged
her to his chest, he drew his gun and smashed her in the
back of the head, knocking her out cold.

"I'm sorry," he said, catching and throwing her over
his shoulder as he started for the entrance to the cave,
"but I'm not about to let you squander your life for crazy
old men."

Clint hurried outside, where he gazed up at the night
sky. The stars were already beginning to fade away, and
it would be touch-and-go whether he could steal past the
Indians and reach his horses before the Indians awoke and
attacked.

"You're going to hate me if we make it out of this
canyon," he said, "but at least you'll be alive to hate me.
If you'd have stayed here, you'd be dead for no reason
at all."

Almost as if she'd heard him, Lucy groaned, and Clint
said a silent prayer that she wouldn't do it again just as he
was trying to sneak past the Indians' camp. Time was running out, but if they didn't get that far they'd never reach
the horses, and the game would be lost for them both.

TWENTY

Clint was damned grateful that he was carrying the unconscious woman down the canyon instead of up it. Still, with dawn already starting to streak the eastern rim of the twisting Grand Canyon, he knew that his precious time was almost over. He still could not believe that Al, Charley, and Pete had refused to at least try to save their own lives, but then gold had always made men crazy.

Clint stayed as distant from the Indian camp as he could, but there was no way that he could sneak past it without being seen if a few warriors were already up and about. So he just grit his teeth and kept moving past the encampment, praying that he could reach the horses and get the hell out of this death trap before it was too late.

Unfortunately, some of the Indians were awake, and when a rock twisted under Clint's boot and dribbled down toward the little running stream, an Indian looked up and saw Clint.

For a frozen moment, they both stared at each other, and then Clint was running as hard as he could for the horses. He heard an Indian shout with alarm, and it was followed by the pounding of running feet. With fire burning in his lungs, Clint kept running, and when he reached Duke, he threw Lucy over the gelding's withers and then climbed on behind her.

"Hiii-yiii!" screamed an Indian as he threw himself at Clint, who yanked his revolver from his holster and shot the man in the chest.

Two more Indians charged, and Clint kicked Duke forward, knocking one spinning and shooting the other Indian in the arm, causing the man to screech in pain.

"Ya, horses!" Clint shouted, trying to hold Lucy across Duke's broad withers and, at the same time, reining the gelding about. He wanted to send him crashing into the horses and make them pull free and race with him for the trail leading up and out of the canyon.

A cloud of arrows sailed over Clint's head as the horses scrambled up the steep trail leading out of the canyon. They ran perhaps a quarter of a mile until the trail narrowed, and then Clint slowed Duke to a walk and dared to take a peek over his shoulder.

The Indian camp had already split into two groups: One group was coming after him, and the other was moving up the side canyon toward the cave in which Pete, Charley, and Al were feverishly digging for Spanish gold.

Lucy moaned and tried to struggle, but Clint gripped her by her belt and shouted, "Hang on and don't move!"

He gave Duke his head, letting his trusted gelding use his own instincts on how best to climb the switching, narrow trail that would bring them back to the rim and offer them a straight run toward Apache Junction.

Clint kept looking over his shoulder. The canyon Indians were wiry and in superb condition, and they were gaining. Clint was not quite sure how they thought they were going to get around all the free horses that were crowding in his wake, also eager to attain the lip of the canyon, but that was their problem. He had problems of his own to worry about. And as for Charley, Pete, and Al, Clint considered them dead men.

"Come on," Clint said, urging Duke up the trail and then deciding that the big horse was carrying too heavy a load up too steep a trail to go any faster.

Clint pulled Duke to a standstill and dismounted. "Wake up, Lucy! You have to sit up and ride. Duke can't carry us both up this cliff fast enough to escape the Indians, and I can't let loose of you or you'll fall."

Lucy moaned, and when Clint got her sitting upright and astride Duke, she finally came fully awake.

"What . . . "

"Don't ask me now," he said, grabbing Duke's reins and pulling the gelding into a trot. "Just hang on!"

"But . . . where's Father!"

Dazed, alarmed, and confused, Lucy tumbled off the horse—fortunately on the cliff side, or she'd have fallen to her death. Clint grabbed her and pulled her to her feet. "I'll explain it later. Come on!"

As if to punctuate the urgency of his words, the lead warrior below fired an arrow that lanced meanly off the rock near their heads. Lucy did not need additional urging. Clint had to keep firing down at the warriors to keep them out of close arrow range.

At last the rim hove into sight, and Clint shouted, "We're going to make it! Don't give up, Lucy!"

"But look!"

Clint did look, and what he saw made his blood run cold. Waiting for them on top with rifles in their fists were none other than Marshal Timberman and six of his bloodthirsty gunslingers.

"What are we going to do!"

Clint glanced back over his shoulder just in time to see another arrow come arcing toward him.

"Duck!" he shouted, dropping to his knees against the cliff wall as Lucy did the same.

At that moment Ulysses Timberman and his men opened fire on the warriors, and their firepower was devastating. At least four Indians died in that first murderous volley, and the rest changed directions to race back down the trail.

"I'd thank Timberman, except I know that he plans to kill us," Clint said.

Lucy's expression was grim. "We can't go back down or the Indians will kill us. I don't know in which direction lies the worst fate."

Clint wiped his perspiring face with the back of his sleeve.

"All I know for sure is that we sure as hell can't stay here."

"Come on up, Gunsmith!" Timberman shouted. "You got nowhere to run or to hide. We can pick you, the woman, and the horses off as easy as fruit from a tree."

"Then do it!" Clint shouted. "But we're the only ones that can help you get that Spanish fortune. We know where it is and how to reach it!"

There was a significant silence, and Clint could almost feel the man above as he weighed the pleasure of killing against the possibility of reaping a fortune.

The fortune won out. "Where is it?"

"You'll have to help us bring it out from down below. Lucy's father and two other prospectors are trapped in a cave where it's buried. We either get them out or it's lost."

"I don't believe you!"

While Clint was trying to figure out his next words, they all heard distant shots echoing up and down the canyons.

"Now do you believe me?"

"What's your deal?"

"Our lives for the treasure."

Timberman waited almost a minute before he spoke. "How do we know that you won't double-cross us?"

"You don't. But we either play it out my way or we all lose. Revenge is sweet, but money is even better. Right?"

"Yeah," Timberman said at last. "All right. We'll play your game."

"Then come on down. We've got some damned angry Indians to drive off."

"Is there enough of us?"

Clint looked up at the rim and counted only Timberman and six others. "What happened to the mayor and his friends?"

"They decided to keep walking," Timberman said with contempt.

"I'll bet," Clint said. "Well, come on down and let's get this over with."

Timberman and his friends disappeared for several minutes, only to reemerge on the trail above. The tall marshal was in front with a Winchester in his fists, and the other men were similarly armed.

Clint had no idea if they were a large enough force to whip the Indians and reach Al, Charley, and Pete, but he figured they'd make a hell of a good try, though for entirely different reasons.

And after they reached the cave—if they did reach it— then they could see about the Spanish gold and who would survive to carry it away.

TWENTY-ONE

They stood on the narrow trail, and as Clint looked into the marshal's eyes, he knew without a doubt that the man wanted more than anything in the world to kill him.

"Your chance will come when this is all over," Clint promised. "There's plenty of time to settle what's between us, but right now, we've got a treasure to uncover and get out of this canyon in one piece."

Timberman struggled to keep control of himself. "Have you seen it?"

"No," Clint said. "They were about to dig into a hidden cavern when I took Lucy and got the hell out of there last night."

"But it's there?"

"Yeah," Clint said. "It's there, all right."

"It better be," Timberman said. "So how many Indians are we going to face?"

Clint shrugged. "At least forty."

"No guns or rifles?"

"Not so far." Clint reloaded his weapons. "There could be other tribes up and down these canyons. I don't know. All I saw was the one camp."

Timberman nodded. "How far are we from the hidden treasure?"

"Five miles at the most."

"Then let's go," Timberman said. "You and the girl in the lead."

"Thanks," Clint said.

The Indians had taken some hard losses and retreated to the bottom of the canyon. When Clint rounded the last bend on the narrow trail, the warriors unleashed a swarm of arrows, and it was all he could do to duck behind a boulder, dragging Duke, Lucy, and her mare to safety.

"Gonna need some firepower up here, boys."

Timberman and his gunhands gathered around.

"Lot of damn Indians," one man said.

"A hell of a lot," another said in a worried voice.

"Shit!" Timberman said with scorn. "They've got arrows and we've got guns and rifles. What in hell is the matter with you boys! Let's mount up and take 'em!"

Clint expelled a deep breath. "I'm not too sure that's the best way to go about it, Marshal."

"Why not!"

"They're pretty accurate with those bows and arrows up close."

Timberman scowled. "If you've got a better plan on how to break through and get to the Spanish fortune, I'm willing to listen."

Clint gave it his best thinking, but in the end he said, "Let's mount up and do it. Lucy, you stay here."

"No! I can ride and shoot too."

"Let her come," Timberman growled. "We'll need every gun we can muster to bust through."

Clint didn't like it, but there was nothing he could do or say to change things, so he tightened his cinch, checked his six-gun once more, and swung into the saddle. Lucy and the other men did the same.

"Any time you're ready, Marshal."

Timberman drew a deep breath. "There sure better be gold waiting for us. There damn sure better!"

Clint only smiled. Suddenly, Timberman let out a yell and was spurring his horse furiously.

The Indians were ready and waiting. Two of Timberman's gunmen died in the first hail of arrows, and a third man was hit in the side but managed to keep his saddle. Clint and Timberman, however, were devastatingly accurate with their fire. They killed six, and the remainder of the hired gunmen proved themselves to be deadly fighters as well.

As they charged through the Indians, shooting and firing, Clint managed to stay near Lucy, and he almost grabbed the bit in her horse's mouth and tried to make a break for freedom, but Lucy anticipated the move and the chance was lost.

The killing was over in less than two minutes, as they raced up the side canyon that Clint had earlier stalked. They did not rein in their horses until they came upon the burros.

"How many did we lose!" Timberman yelled, twisting around in his saddle.

"Two men! Red is hurt pretty bad."

The man named Red was bent over in his saddle, swaying and trying to stop the blood from flowing out of his side. Timberman went over to him and asked, "You gonna be able to make it?"

"Yeah," Red grunted. "I sure as hell ain't got no choice."

"You're right about that," Timberman said, without even offering to try and stop the bleeding. "Maybe the woman can put a bandage around that hole."

Lucy rode over, and Clint helped her get Red out of his

saddle. They laid the gunman down, and Clint ripped open his shirt. The arrowhead was still embedded in the man's side. Clint grabbed the stump of the shaft and pulled the arrow out, causing Red to faint.

"Bandage him up," Timberman ordered. "If he can help us when we break out of here, then we'll take him back. Otherwise . . ."

Clint did not have to ask what the "otherwise" meant. Timberman would leave Red behind to be scalped alive if he thought the man would serve no good purpose.

When the bandaging was done and there was nothing more that could be done for Red, Timberman pointed toward the cavern. "Is that it?"

"Yeah," Clint said.

Timberman raised the barrel of his rifle and pointed it at Clint's chest. "Then unholster your gun with your left hand and throw it down before you enter."

Clint had expected such a demand. One thing for sure: Timberman was holding the high cards, and he'd have been a fool not to play them. Even now, the other gunmen were turning their weapons on him and Lucy.

Clint threw down his gun. "Nice to be among such trusting men," he said dryly.

"Lead the way into the cave," Timberman said. "We'll be right behind you."

Clint took Lucy's arm. He didn't think that their odds of survival were much improved over an hour before, when he and the woman had been trapped on the cliff between Timberman and the Indians. But the odds sure weren't any worse, either. And if they could just find some gold, then maybe in their excitement, Timberman and his three remaining hired guns would get careless. The only problem was that they all needed each other to get out of this mess alive, with or without the Spanish gold.

TWENTY-TWO

Timberman posted two men outside to guard against an Indian attack.

"All right," he said, waving his six-gun in the general direction of Clint and Lucy's chest. "We've wasted too much time already. Inside!"

Clint was worried that Timberman would gun him and the woman down the moment they found the treasure—if indeed there really was a fortune in Spanish gold up ahead.

"Just remember that we need each other to get out of this canyon alive. Treasure or no treasure."

"I'll try to keep that in mind," Timberman said. "Now move!"

Clint took Lucy's hand, and together they walked deeper into the cave. They had scarcely walked more than a few yards before they heard the excited voices of Al and Pete. Then Clint heard a high burst of laughter.

"They've found it!" Lucy cried, rushing forward with Clint on her heels.

They burst into the cavern to see the two old prospectors in the act of dragging a small, old metal-ribbed chest from the rubble of what appeared to be the opening of another cavern.

"Hold it!" Timberman shouted, rushing past Clint with his gun in his fist. "I want that!"

Al wore a dazed expression, and it seemed to take him a moment to comprehend that he was about to be robbed of this long anticipated moment.

"What the devil!" he cried, staggering to his feet, the box clutched to his bony chest.

"Give it to me, or so help me I'll blow your brains all over that rock pile," Timberman warned, cocking back the hammer of his gun.

"No!"

Timberman would have shot the old prospector if Lucy had not thrown herself forward to protect her father.

"Give it to him!" she cried, wrenching the chest from his hands and throwing it at Timberman.

Al almost went crazy. The old man cursed and tried to reach the box, but Clint stepped up and caught him with an uppercut to the jaw that knocked him out cold.

"Do you have to keep doing that to people!" Lucy cried.

Clint rubbed his knuckles. "Sometimes it's the only way to save a fool's life."

Lucy knelt beside her father. She glared at Clint and then at Timberman. "Why don't you take it and get out of here!"

In answer, Timberman snatched up the box. It was padlocked, and he tried to tear the lock free, but it held solid. In anger, he hurled the box against the wall, and when it still did not open, he shot the lock apart. Everyone crowded around it as Timberman opened the box.

"Gold!" he cried, digging his hands into the small round Spanish coins. "Gold and silver!"

Everyone gaped at the coins, and as they did, Clint stepped over to one man and tore his gun loose.

"Hold it!" he shouted. "First man moves, he's dead!"

Timberman's gun was still in his own fist, and he leveled it at Lucy. "I'll put a bullet through her heart before I die. So what's it to be?"

Clint expelled a deep breath. "Maybe it's time you and I decided who's going to take over. That's what I'd like; only I don't think you've got the guts for it."

Timberman sneered. "I hate Wallace Boggs, but he told me before we started out here that only a fool would risk his life against a man like you for pride. Well, I'm no fool. So put your gun away, Mr. Adams. We'll settle up after we get out of this canyon. We need each other."

Clint hated the idea of putting his gun away. But at least now he was armed and therefore he had a chance. Under any other circumstances, he would have killed Ulysses Timberman.

"All right," he said finally. "But as soon as we are out of this canyon and safe on the rim, I'm either going to kill you, or you're going to kill me."

"Fair enough," Timberman said.

Pete seemed to snap out of his own trance. "I think there's more. A lot more!"

Suddenly, everyone's attention was focused on the old man. "What makes you think that?" Clint asked.

Pete turned toward the cavern. "I just do. I think there's a fortune buried up ahead and that this is only part of it."

"How do you know that?" Timberman demanded.

Pete swallowed nervously. He was covered with rock dust, and his fingernails were ripped and bleeding. Clint thought the man looked crazy as a loon.

"I just got a hunch, is all."

"A hunch?"

"Yeah. Al and I talked about it. This loose rock we been diggin' at must have all dropped over the opening. You can see how it musta, can't you, Marshal?"

Timberman, along with all of them, glanced up at the rock walls. "I can't tell any damn thing," he swore. "I'm no miner."

"Well, just look at it," Pete said, pointing to the rock formation. "See how this place we was diggin' is all loose rock and how it forms a tunnel like?"

"Yeah, I guess so."

"Well, down this tunnel is where we think there's a lot more treasure, and—"

Suddenly they heard a shout: "Marshal, the Indians are coming!"

Pete's words were instantly forgotten, as everyone turned and stampeded back toward the entrance to the tunnel.

"Looks like they got some reinforcements," Timberman said.

Clint agreed. They could see the Indians were gathering into a large attacking force.

The man who had been assigned to watch their horses and the burros asked, "What are we gonna do, Marshal?"

"We can hold them off as long as we need to," Timberman said. "We've got some food, and this stream is all the water we need."

Timberman went over to his horse and yanked his Winchester from his saddle boot. He knelt on one knee, took aim, and fired. The distance was well over four hundred yards, and it seemed to take about two beats of Clint's heart before he saw an Indian scream and grab his belly, then flop into the dirt, rolling and shrieking in pain.

"Nice damn shooting," a man said in admiration, as the Indians scattered for cover.

It had been nice shooting, but it disgusted Clint. The belly-shot Indian was going to die a horrible, agonizing death. Clint would not have gut-shot a wild animal that way, much less a human being.

"Here," Timberman said to the man he'd stationed outside. "They get excited again, see if you can do the same as I just did."

"I'm not that good with a rifle."

Timberman yanked his Winchester away from the man. "Who is a marksman?"

"I am," one of them said.

"Then you wait out here and pick them off whenever they get into range."

Clint went over to Red. The man was conscious now, and Clint gave him a drink of water from his canteen.

"Thanks," Red told him with pain-glazed eyes. "Am I going to die?"

"I don't know," Clint said. "But I think you probably are."

The man's eyes squeezed shut, and they were wet when they reopened. "What about the Spanish fortune? You find any?"

"A little. Maybe a thousand dollars or two worth of old coins."

"That's all?"

"Yeah." Clint studied the cliffs around them. They were impossible to scale. There was no way out this side canyon except the way they'd come in, and this time the Indians were going be a lot better prepared against guns and rifles.

"Hey listen, Gunsmith," Red whispered. "I'm sorry that we were on opposite sides of this thing. It was just a case of Boggs paying my freight."

"I know."

"You won't leave me alive for them to scalp or—"

"No," Clint said. "I won't do that."

Timberman came over and knelt beside Red. "You look like death to me," he told the man.

Red coughed, and his face twisted in anger. "When it's time to go," he said through clenched teeth, "you tie me in my saddle, and I'll damn sure take a few of those heathen bastards with me before I cash in my chips."

Timberman studied Red's face. "We'll see," he said. "If you're still alive when we ride, we'll just see."

When Timberman had posted his guard and hurried back inside the tunnel, Clint looked over at the guard and asked, "Any whiskey among you?"

"The marshal keeps some in his saddlebags. I drank all mine the first night on the trail. So did the others."

Clint went over to Timberman's horse and tore open the man's saddlebags, extracting a half-pint of whiskey.

"You better not do that," the guard warned. "When he finds out you took his drink, he'll—"

"He'll what? Kill me? He's already planning to try to do that the minute we are out of this canyon," Clint said, taking the whiskey over to Red and kneeling beside him.

"Here," Clint said, giving the man the bottle. "Finish it as you need to."

"Thanks," Red told him with obvious gratitude. His face was white and covered with sweat. He looked to be in tremendous pain, and there wasn't a damn thing anyone could do about it.

Clint nodded and walked slowly to the mouth of the tunnel. "Keep them back at least to those trees off to the right of the canyon," he said.

"I will," the guard promised. "But if you hear me shootin' fast, come running."

"Count on that," Clint told the man as he went back inside the tunnel.

When he returned to the cavern, there was a spirited debate going on between Timberman, who wanted to keep digging, and another of his gunmen named Bill, who thought that Pete's theory of more gold was pure bullshit.

"That loose rock may be a hundred feet deep!" Bill argued. "We could spend weeks digging for nothing!"

"Yeah," the marshal said, "but there ain't but a few thousand dollars worth of gold in the box. That sure as hell ain't no fortune. I say we at least dig until tonight. If we don't find any more gold, then we break and run for the rim."

Bill kept glancing toward the tunnel's entrance. It was obvious that he wanted to get out of this place with his life more than he needed to find additional treasure.

Timberman turned to Clint. "What do you think?"

Surprised to be asked his opinion, Clint smiled. "I doubt we'd stand a chance of getting past those Indians in daylight. Given that it's still early afternoon, why not dig farther?"

"See!" Timberman said. "Even the Gunsmith agrees with me."

"Well, he don't know any more than we do about mining!"

Timberman's patience ran out. He grabbed Bill by the shirtfront and said, "Goddamn you, we're going to stay here and dig!"

Bill tore free. His fear of Timberman was sufficiently motivating to cause him to drop to his knees and start digging.

"Old man," Timberman said to Pete, "get back to work."

Pete hurried up to the wall of loose rock. "I'd give anything for a damn shovel," he said as he started to dig. "Or even a pair of good leather gloves."

"Any chance of more of this stuff breaking free from up above?" Bill asked, with unconcealed anxiety.

Pete looked up at the roof. "Sure there is."

"Well, how will we know when it's going to happen?"

"You won't." Pete kept digging. "But if it does and it lands on us, we sure as hell won't have to worry about the Indians or any other damn thing."

Bill shot a nervous glance toward the mouth of the tunnel. "That's what I keep telling myself. I mean, all the treasure in the world ain't going to do us any good if we get ourselves filled with arrows."

Clint and Lucy looked at each other. Her father was just starting to come awake from the blow that Clint had administered, and the Gunsmith could see that Lucy was truly frightened. The man was right: You couldn't spend a fortune if you were dead.

TWENTY-THREE

When Al regained consciousness, he watched everyone digging furiously at the loose rock, for a moment, and then he also went to work.

"I'm sorry I had to hit you," Clint said.

"You saved my life, didn't you?"

"I did."

"Well then, don't be sorry," Al snapped. "Because it was a damn fine punch, and I needed it to knock some sense into my head."

"Shut up and dig over there," Timberman hissed.

Clint dug along with the rest of them, Lucy included. Like the others, he had a hunch that old Pete and Al could smell gold somewhere just ahead, but he had his doubts as to whether they could reach it soon enough.

"Hey," Bill shouted, recoiling in horror. "Look!"

They all stared at the bashed-in crown of a man's skull, encased in a leather hat so rotted that it had less strength than a sheet of wet paper.

"Jeezus!" Pete breathed. "What happened to him?"

Clint carefully brushed the rotted leather aside to study the skull. He slipped his index finger through the shattered crown and said, "The man was brained by a sharp instrument. Some kind of an Indian war club, unless I miss my guess."

"Should we go on?" Pete asked.

"Hell yes we go on!" Timberman shouted. "Who cares about a damned old Spanish skeleton?"

Clint looked at the others as they started to uncover the skeleton. The man's clothes were also rotted over his bones, and he was weaponless. The only thing of any interest were the brass buttons on his shirt, and Lucy kept them for herself because they weren't worth anything except for their historical value.

"He was a short bastard, wasn't he," Timberman said to no one in particular, as he grabbed the bones and started tossing them aside.

No one had a reply, and when the bones were gone, they dug even faster, scooping away the loose rock that kept sliding down from the pile.

The hours passed quickly until another body was discovered.

"This one died the same way as the other," Clint said, tracing the broken edges of the skull.

"Who gives a damn!" Timberman swore in anger. "All I want to know is when are we going to break through to the treasure!"

No one could answer the question. After a long while, Clint pushed to his feet. "I'm going out to check on Red and the Indian situation."

"Not alone you ain't!" Timberman jumped to his feet and dusted his hands on his shirt and pants. "The rest of you keep digging while we go outside."

Lucy said nothing, and neither did the three old prospectors. But Bill was a complainer. "My back feels like it's broken already. We been at this for hours! I need a break too."

"Dig, damn you!" Timberman swore.

Bill opened his mouth to argue, but Timberman's expression changed his mind and he kept digging.

Clint was covered with rock dust and bone-tired as he made his way back to the mouth of the tunnel. The guard turned sharply when they emerged.

"Anything happening down there?" Clint asked, studying the Indians.

"Not yet. They seem confused. The marshal's last rifle bullet really put the fear in their hearts."

Timberman studied the gathering of Indians. They all had bows and arrows; a few carried spears. Some shouted and pointed.

"I doubt," Clint said dryly, "that they're inviting us to supper."

"That's for damn sure. But as long as they're down there and we've got a good field of fire, I think we're safe enough. They might be able to charge up and overrun us, but we'd take about twenty or thirty with us, and I doubt they're that eager to die."

Clint shook his head. "On the surface, I'd agree. However, we have one real weak spot in our defense."

"What the hell are you talking about?" Timerman demanded, obviously annoyed at the thought he might have overlooked a chink in their defense. "We got cliffs to our backs, and this is a box canyon. I don't see any way we cannot be safe, as long as we hole up in that tunnel and keep our horses and them burros picketed real close behind the rocks."

"What about up above?" Clint said, taking great care not to look up.

Timberman and the guard, however, both craned their heads upward.

"Don't do that, dammit!" Clint said. "You'll give them ideas."

Both men snapped their chins down. "What the hell do you mean?"

"I mean that if I was them, I'd be on my way up to the rim of this canyon. From up above, they could either roll rocks down on us or make fires and shove burning logs and brush down on us."

"So what?" the guard said. "We just sit back in that cave and watch the fire show."

Timberman shook his head. "You dumb sonofabitch, you don't get it, do you? They roll boulders down or throw burning logs, do you really think our horses and them burros are gonna stick around no matter how strong that picket line? Hell, they'd either be killed or they'll stampede down the canyon and we'll be afoot. Then how will we get the hell out of here?"

Clint studied the entrance to the cave. It was no more than three feet tall and it would be impossible to get their horses inside, though the burros were another story.

"Are you thinking what I'm thinking?" Timberman said.

"That we ought to throw those four burros and drag them inside?"

"Yeah," Timberman said. "If everything went to hell, we could slaughter and eat them. There's that little stream so we'd have both food and water. There's no way that the Indians could get down the tunnel to us. We'd kill them faster than they could come."

Clint wasn't too sure if that were true or not but he, like Ulysses Timberman, had learned to plan for the worst, and bringing the burros inside and tying them down where they could not run away or be hurt made good sense.

"I'll get Bill to help us," Timberman said, disappearing into the tunnel.

Clint went over to kneel beside Red. "I see you're still enjoying the view," he said, trying to make a joke.

"Will you shoot me, Gunsmith?" Red asked weakly. "That whiskey is all gone, and I'm just sufferin' my way into the grave."

The man grabbed Clint's wrist. "I want you to shoot me in the head."

"I can't do that."

"You got to! I ain't makin' it out of here alive, and I'm more scared of fallin' into the hands of those murderin' savages than I am of dying."

Clint looked into the man's suffering eyes. "I won't let the Indians take you alive, Red. I promise."

But Red shook his head. "That's a promise we both know you can't keep if things get bad and there's Indians swarming over us. Kill me!"

Clint looked away and thought about it for a minute. The man was dying very badly and, had their situations been reversed, Clint guessed he'd probably want the same quick end.

"Here," he said, unholstering his gun.

Red nodded and blinked away tears. "I am damned sorry for the grief I helped bring upon you."

"Forget it."

"No. I want you to have my share of the treasure. It's the only thing I got left to give you, and it's yours."

"Thanks," Clint said.

"What the hell is he talking about?" Timberman asked, coming up behind Clint. "And what's he holding a gun for?"

"I gave it to him," Clint explained. "He thinks he's suffered enough."

Red nodded his head. "Marshal, I told the Gunsmith he can have my share of the fortune. I'm giving it to him.

You understand me?"

"He's gettin' nothing but a bullet when we get free of this canyon," Timberman snarled.

"He gets my share!"

"You're a dead man! I don't make deals with dead men," Timberman snarled as he turned away.

Red's face twisted with rage. "Then neither do I!" he cried hoarsely, as he thumbed back the hammer of his gun and shot Timberman in the small of his back.

The marshal raised up on his toes and tried desperately to reach behind his back, as if he could pull the bullet out of himself. Red shot Timberman again between the shoulder blades, and the marshal crashed to the ground, feet kicking for a moment, before the air went out of his lungs and he died.

Then, before Clint could stop him, Red opened his mouth and blew his brains out.

The three shots were not spaced by three seconds. The guard stood with his mouth hanging open and was too stunned to move, until Clint snatched his gun back from Red and pointed it at the man and said, "You take my orders now or you take my bullet. Your choice— make it!"

The guard's hands flew up over his head. "Don't kill me!"

Clint lowered his gun. "I couldn't even if I wanted to. We're down to just you, me, and Bill who are any good with guns. The odds are already mighty slim, and I'm not about to make them any slimmer."

The guard expelled a visible sigh of relief. He stared at the body of Ulysses Timberman. "I hated that bastard," he said, more to himself than to Clint. "Me and the others talked about it, and we knew that he'd try to kill us once we got the gold up to the rim. He'd have killed everybody if he could have, just to keep the gold for himself."

"He'd have tried, all right," Clint said in agreement.

"What the—"

Clint spun around, and the gun in his hand was up and steady on Bill's chest. "Timberman is dead. You want to join him—or me?"

"Don't shoot me!" Bill cried. "All I want is to get out of here alive! That's what I been saying since we been down in this hell."

Clint lowered his pistol. "Let's get the burros thrown and tied. It'll take all three of us to drag them one by one into the tunnel."

Bill swallowed. "You killed 'em both, huh?"

"No," Clint said. "Red shot the marshal, and then he killed himself."

"But why?"

"Let him tell you," Clint said, as he went to his horse for a rope. "And let's get busy!"

When Clint untied his rope, he sneaked a glance up at the rim and, sure enough, he thought he saw some movement. He crouched behind Duke so that he could not be seen by the Indians down the canyon, and then he took his time scanning the rim above. Unfortunately, he couldn't see much, because daylight was quickly fading and the cliff overhead was so steep that he had a very narrow angle of perspective.

"Are they up there?" the guard asked, following Clint's eyes.

"If they aren't now, they will be soon," Clint predicted, "so let's not waste any more time gawking."

"Why don't we just get the hell out of here right now!"

Clint reckoned that was not such an all-fired bad idea. "Let's forget the burros," he said, retying his rope. "Come full dark, we're riding for our lives."

Bill nodded. "Thank God Ulysses Timberman is dead. You're the only man among us that has talked any sense from the moment we came down that mountain-goat trail into this hell."

Clint started to say something, but a sudden movement on the rim caught his eye. "Look!"

Bill and the gunman both saw the movement too.

"Six or seven Indians," Clint said. "They're still three or four miles from being over us, but it won't take them long."

"Will they be over us before sundown?" Bill asked.

"If they are, we're going to be in a hell of a fix," Clint said, and he turned and rushed back into the tunnel to tell the others they were leaving just as soon as the sun went down and the shadows faded into an inky darkness.

TWENTY-FOUR

"You can stop digging," Clint said, "because we're leaving in about thirty minutes—even less, if I think it's dark enough to give us a slim chance of breaking out of this canyon."

Al, Charley, and Pete looked up, and their old faces were alive with excitement. "Look!" Al whispered. "Look at what we just found!"

Clint walked over and knelt beside the prospector. The pine torches that had given them light all day now had began to flicker. Still, they gave Clint sufficient light to see the gold coins piled in Al's big hand.

"There's one under every damned rock!" Pete cried, pulling handfuls out of his pockets.

Even Lucy seemed oblivious of every danger now. "Clint," she said with excitement, "the entire fortune must be within arm's reach of us!"

"You've got fifteen minutes," Clint said, dropping the gold coins in the dust and turning back toward the mouth of the canyon. "In fifteen minutes we're breaking out of here, and we've got to do it together or we'll all die."

"I'm not going anyplace," Al swore. "Not until we've

177

uncovered this. We need a few more hours, and we'll be rich!"

"Damn you!" Clint raged. "In a few more hours our horses will either be roasted or run off, and we'll be doomed! You've got fifteen minutes while I check the cinches and prepare to break out of here."

Clint started to stomp out of the dim cavern, but Lucy overtook him. "They'll be ready," she said. "I swear they will."

But Clint shook his head. "They've gone mad," he said. "They've completely lost their senses over this gold."

"I'll *make* them listen to reason," Lucy vowed. "I swear that I will!"

The anger went out of Clint. "You'll try," he said. "But I don't give you much chance of succeeding."

Lucy stuffed her hands into Clint's pockets and filled them with gold coins. "If we don't make it—and you do—I want you to have something to remember me by."

Clint took Lucy into his arms and kissed her mouth. "You're going to make it. And anyway, it wouldn't be gold that I remembered a woman like you by. It would be much, much more than that."

"Why didn't we make love since the last time?"

"I don't know," he confessed. "I guess that gold fever got in our way."

"Yeah." Lucy pushed out of his arms and went back to her father, Charley, and Pete.

"They'll be ready," she called, as Clint hurried outside to make his preparations. "They'll be ready!"

Once outside, the first thing that Clint did was to look up at the rim. He couldn't see the Indians, but that gave him no comfort because he knew without the slightest doubt that they were up there and that they'd be preparing to bombard their enemies just as soon as they could gather rocks or brush and get it burning.

"Let's check all the cinches," he ordered.

"What about the burros?" Bill asked. "What about them?"

"We stampede them before us. They can't hurt us, and they might add to the general confusion. We'll also drive the loose horses in front of us. The more things we can get moving down that canyon, the better our chances."

The other gunman stared down at the Indians. "I don't think we can do it a second time with so few guns. I think we're going to die."

"Then *don't* think," Clint said angrily, as he watered the horses and checked their cinches. "Because wrong thinking gets a man killed for certain."

"Are they coming?" Bill asked, looking toward the cavern.

"I don't know," Clint confessed.

"We sure could use their guns, even if they can't shoot."

"I know," Clint said roughly.

Fifteen minutes later, the sun was gone and the shadows were being swallowed by a thick darkness.

"Mount up," Clint ordered. "I'll go inside and get them, and we'll ride for it."

A rock tumbled down from high above. It struck about twenty yards down the canyon, but it was close enough to cause the burros and the horses to jump with fright.

"You better hurry," Bill said. "I got a feeling that we are going to get rained on any damn minute!"

Clint rushed into the cavern to hear Lucy pleading with her father, Charley, and Pete.

"We have to go *now*! All of us!"

"You go," Al swore. "We're staying."

"We need you to help us to escape! We have to do this

all together, Father. If we don't, none of us have any chance!"

"She's right," Clint said, watching the three old men stuff their packs to bulging. "You must each have thousands of dollars worth of gold in those packs. We can't haul out any more. So come on!"

"No!" Pete shouted. "There's a fortune here to be taken and—"

Clint jumped forward, rushed across the cavern, and backhanded Pete across the mouth so hard that the old man's head snapped like a whip. Then he did the same to Al, breaking the man's lips. Charley backed away to avoid the vicious back hand.

"If you want to throw your lives away, then good riddance!" Clint shouted. "But now you're also throwing away mine and Lucy's! That's not right!"

Al's head wagged back and forth. His tongue came out and tasted blood. "He's right, Pete. We got enough."

"But—"

"We can come back again some day!" Al shouted. "We can come back!"

Pete's chin dipped to his chest. "I ain't ever coming back, not in this life," he said. "And I don't think you are either. We still ain't going to be rich; not like we wanted."

Al pushed to his feet, and the hardness went out of his voice. "We'll be rich enough. Besides, if we was real rich, we'd never go prospecting again, now would we?"

Pete blinked in slow comprehension. "Yeah," he whispered, "that's right. We never would."

"Then let's ride for our lives."

Clint exchanged weary smiles with Lucy, and they both helped the three crazy old prospectors carry their heavy packs of Spanish gold.

When they emerged from the cavern it was dark, and

Bill was almost fit to be tied.

"They're startin' a fire up there above us! Look at the embers!"

Clint stepped out from the canyon wall and gazed up at the distant bonfire. Embers were sailing up into the night.

"They're about to push it over," he said in a tight voice. "Let's mount up and ride!"

No one had to be told twice. The packs of gold were thrown over saddlehorns and they were mounted in an instant.

"If any of us goes down, the rest just keep going as hard and fast down this canyon as you can. Once out of it, we hit the Colorado and turn east. Two miles farther we come to the only trail that will deliver us from this hell. Everyone got that straight?"

No one answered, but Clint figured that was because they were all thinking about how bad their chances were of making it out alive.

"Here it comes!" Al shouted.

Their heads snapped up, and they saw a huge fireball edge over the lip of the rim and start to come rolling down upon them.

Clint drew his six-gun—there were two more stuffed behind his belt—and he opened fire, sending the burros and the extra horses jumping forward to stampede down the canyon. "Let's go!" Clint shouted, putting his heels to Duke's flanks and sending the big gelding leaping forward.

Clint made damn sure that Lucy was right beside him as they crowded the slower horses and burros. He felt his back scorched as the fireball struck the canyon floor and exploded with burning embers and the entire box canyon was suddenly as light as if it were full day.

In that one second of brilliant illumination, Clint looked

around to see everyone's faces, and he had the satisfaction
of knowing that, while they might not survive the next few
seconds, they'd every last one of them go down fighting.

Clint had been in some hard, desperate situations, but
this was one of the worst. As soon as the light from the
fire died, the canyon was plunged back into total darkness.
Yet he knew that the Indians had seen them coming and
would be firing blindly into the path. The poor burros and
spare horses would take the first deadly volley, and for
that reason, Clint reined Duke back.

He guessed they ran about three hundred yards when the
line of running horses and burros ahead of them suddenly
began to fall like dominoes. The burros were the first to
drop, but the horses, still wearing their saddles, had more
protection; and, being stronger, they raced on, except for
a few that were hit with arrows that drove deep into their
chests.

When the horse in front of him went down, Clint opened
fire, and the sound of his gun was signal enough to start
the rest of them shooting.

The next minute seemed to last forever. It was a blind
chaos. Clint emptied his gun, threw it away, pulled another from his waistband, and emptied it before grabbing his
own six-gun.

He heard screams in the night. He felt Duke almost lose
his footing as the powerful gelding struck an invisible warrior and broke him like a rag doll, leaving him trampled
underfoot.

An arrow hit him in the arm, but he tore it from his flesh
and raced on. He heard Al or Pete cry out in pain and one
of the horses scream as it went down. Lucy also screamed,
but he could not even see, much less help her.

And then, just as suddenly as the nightmare had begun,
it was over, and they had broken through the Indian camp

and were racing toward the Colorado. The canyon opened a little, and faint moonlight guided Clint to the east and across a deep bed of sand that made Duke work hard.

Clint looked over his shoulder to see Lucy hanging onto a gun in one fist, her saddlehorn in the other. One gunman had passed through the terrible gauntlet, and it was Bill. Pete and Charley were gone, their riderless horses identifiable because of the heavy packs of gold tied to the saddlehorns. Al was bent over in his saddle and still riding hard.

"The trail's just up ahead," Clint shouted, driving the surviving saddle horses ahead of him.

When they finally passed the armor-wearing tree and cut sharply to their right, the trail seemed as if it were drenched in moonlight, a golden path lifting upward to life.

Duke took that path, and so did the others. And somehow they reached the top, to rein their horses to a trembling, sweaty standstill.

Lucy rushed into Clint's arms, sobbing with relief and gratitude. Bill helped Al down from his horse and said, "He's just nicked up a little, same as all the rest of us. More scared than anything else."

Clint held Lucy in his arms. "We've got the gold."

"But we lost Pete and Charley."

"Maybe they wanted to die rich men," Clint said. "Let's get ourselves patched up and put some miles between us and the Grand Canyon. We can change to the extra horses and give our own some easier miles."

"What are you going to do when you see Mayor Boggs again?" Lucy asked. "He'll be waiting in Apache Junction with his men."

"They're all dead," Bill said. "The marshal found them up on the rim as we was backtracking. Boggs was too weak to walk any farther, so Timberman put him out of his misery. The others were only a few miles on, and Timberman shot them too."

Clint looked over at the gunmen. "But you had no part in that?"

"No. I'm not a murderer."

Clint believed Bill. "Then it's all over," he said, staring at the two bulging packs of Spanish gold pieces. "And I guess that we're as rich as we'll probably ever be."

All four of them gazed at the bulging packs, but no one seemed excited or even happy. The price of the Grand Canyon gold, it seemed obvious, had just been too damned high.

A special offer for people who enjoy reading the best Westerns published today. If you enjoyed this book, subscribe now and get . . .

TWO FREE WESTERNS!
A $5.90 VALUE—NO OBLIGATION

If you enjoyed this book and would like to read more of the very best Westerns being published today, you'll want to subscribe to True Value's Western Home Subscription Service. If you enjoyed the book you just read and want more of the most exciting, adventurous, action packed Westerns, subscribe now.

TWO FREE BOOKS

When you subscribe, we'll send you your first month's shipment of the newest and best 6 Westerns for you to preview. With your first shipment, two of these books will be yours as our introductory gift to you absolutely FREE, regardless of what you decide to do.

Special Subscriber Savings

As a True Value subscriber all regular monthly selections will be billed at the low subscriber price of just $2.45 each. That's at least a savings of $3.00 each month below the publishers price. There is never any shipping, handling or other hidden charges. What's more there is no minimum number of books you must buy, you may return any selection for full credit and you can cancel your subscription at any time. A TRUE VALUE!

∼ Mail the coupon below ∼

To start your subscription and receive 2 FREE WESTERNS, fill out the coupon below and mail it today. We'll send you your first shipment which includes 2 FREE BOOKS as soon as we receive it.